The W

Tw

A hit WITHDRAWN

"Will whet appetites of fans of both *Iron Chef* and

wine, and winemaking, and the whole culture of that fascinating world. And then I find it's the first of a series. I can see myself enjoying many a bottle of wine while enjoying the adventures of Benjamin Cooker in this terrific new series."

—*William Martin, New York Times bestselling author*

"An excellent mystery series in which you eat, drink and discuss wine as much as you do murders."

—*Bernard Frank, Le Nouvel Observateur*

"Perfect for people who might like a little treachery with their evening glass of Bordeaux, a little history and tradition with their Merlot."

—*AustCrime*

"A wonderful translation... wonderful descriptions of the art, architecture, history and landscape of the Bordeaux region... The shoes are John Lobb, the cigars are Cuban, and the wine is 'classic.' As is this book."

—*Rantin', Ravin' and Reading*

"Combines a fairly simple mystery with the rich feel of the French winemaking industry. The descriptions of the wine and the food are mouth-watering!"

—*The Butler Did It*

"Benjamin Cooker uses his composure, erudition and intuition to solve heady crimes that take place in the exclusive—and realistic—world of grand cru wines."

—*Jean-Claude Raspiengeas, La Croix*

"An enjoyable, quick read with the potential for developing into a really unique series."

—*Rachel Coterill Book Reviews*

"A fine vintage forged by the pens of two very different varietals. It is best consumed slightly chilled, and never alone. You will be intrigued by its mystery, and surprised by its finish, and it will stay with you for a very long time."

—*Peter May, prize-winning, international bestselling author*

"A series that is both delectable for connoisseurs of wine and an initiation for those not in the know."

—*Marine de Tilly, Le Figaro*

"I finished it in one sitting! I learned so much about wine making... But more than that is was a good little mystery—nothing wasted. The book would be perfect for a book club to have a 'wine' night."

—*Bless Your Hearts Mom*

"This is an excellent translation. You never have the feeling you are reading a translated text. The author obviously knows Bordeaux extremely well, and he knows quite a bit about oenology. The book should be a hit with lovers of Bordeaux wine."

—*Tom Fiorini, The Vine Route*

Grand Cru Heist

A Winemaker Detective Novel

Jean-Pierre Alaux
&
Noël Balen

Translated from French by Anne Trager

LE FRENCH BOOK

First published in France as
Pour qui sonne l'angélus
by Jean-Pierre Alaux and Noël Balen

First published in English in 2013
By Le French Book, Inc., New York
www.lefrenchbook.com

Copyediting by Amy Richards
Cover designed by David Zampa
Proofreading by Chris Gage
E-book designed by Le French Book

ISBNs:
Trade paperback: 978-1-939474-04-9
Hardcover: 978-1-939474-12-4
E-Book: 978-1-939474-08-7

*"Finishing off a bottle of wine together
is a fine sign of friendship."*
—Jean Carmet

1

Paris finally returned to its splendor at dusk. Lights from the cruise boats caressed the buildings on the Left Bank. The bridges cast wavering shadows on the waters of the Seine. At the corner of the Rue Dauphine, a few patches of half-melted snow, curiously saved from the passing footsteps, were shining under the streetlights.

Benjamin Cooker had felt deprived of light all day. He awaited this miraculous hour, when everything could be reborn in the fleeting glow of night. As he got older, he had less tolerance for the unchanging leaden sky that covered Paris in winter. Everything, from the pallid faces of café servers to the hotel concierge's waxy complexion, the bare trees in the Tuileries Gardens, and the homeless camping out on the subway grates, seemed dull and gray. He had loved this city in his happy-go-lucky days, and now he found it suffocating.

Here, even the snow was hoary, dirty, and reduced to mud in a few hours with the constant comings and goings of the city. He missed peaceful Médoc, and he was impatient to return to his home, Grangebelle, the next day. The vineyards would be superb, all white and wrapped in silence. The cold would be dry and refreshing, and the sky nearly royal blue. He would go for a solitary walk along the Gironde just to hear the snow crunch under his boots. Elisabeth got cold easily and would probably remain in front of the fire in the living room, her hands around a steaming cup of tea.

Benjamin Cooker drove slowly, letting his gloves glide over the steering wheel while he whistled along with a Chopin nocturne on the radio. According to the too-ceremonious radio host, it was *Opus 19*. He was comfortable, settled into the leather seat of his classic Mercedes 280SL. He turned onto Pont des Arts to get to his hotel, which was near the opera house. The red light was taking forever. He lifted the collar of his Loden and turned up the radio as someone approached the car, flicking his thumb to mimic a lighter. Cooker squinted to get a better look at the man's face. It was hidden under a hood, but he seemed young, despite his stooped, somewhat misshapen form. Cooker shook his head and waved his hands to indicate that he did not smoke.

The light turned green, but Cooker did not have time to accelerate. His car door opened suddenly, as if it had been ripped off, and cold air rushed in.

"Take that, rich bastard."

The man pulled out a switchblade. Cooker did not move. *Don't panic. Stay calm. Breathe slowly. Think fast.* He felt the tip of the knife on his Adam's apple and gulped. A second man opened the other door and searched the glove compartment.

"Get rid of him," he said, unbuckling Cooker's seat belt.

The hooded man hit Cooker twice in the jaw, grabbed him by the tie, and dragged him to the ground. Then the thug kicked him in the stomach, head, and ribs—"Take that, asshole." The taste of blood and thick grit from the pavement burned his lips—"Your mother's a bitch." A final glance, a few notes of Chopin—"Eat shit, dirtbag!"—and screeching tires. Then nothing.

§ § §

Staff hurried through the corridors at the Pitié-Salpetrière Hospital. The warm aroma of hot coffee filled the ward. Benjamin Cooker was trying to look at the small corner of white sky that

3

was attempting—in vain—to light up the room, but he could barely turn his head.

"Don't worry, sir. You're safe here."

The nurse had bright green eyes. A gold cross was hanging from her beautiful freckled neck. She had a soft voice; it was almost tender and sleep-inducing.

"You should get some rest. You are still in shock, Mr. Cooker. Your wife will be here soon."

She spoke the way a child would speak to her father. Cooker thought about his daughter, Margaux. He hoped that Elisabeth had not told her what had happened. There was no sense causing worry. He could barely remember anything from the previous night, except the 1961 Latour he had shared with Claude Nithard, his publisher, at the Tour d'Argent.

The nurse took his pulse, explaining that he had been found unconscious on the sidewalk and rushed to the emergency room.

"What about my car?"

"Stay calm, sir. It is only a car. You are lucky to be alive."

A tear rolled down Cooker's cheek. He closed his eyes and sighed deeply to expel the feeling of powerless rage and isolation that tightened his chest. His old convertible also carried his tawny leather briefcase, which held the fountain pen Margaux had given him. A jeweler in New York had engraved his name on it. The briefcase also held some bank statements, his agenda, and the thick dog-eared notebook he was very attached to. Year after year, the winemaker had jotted down his impressions of all the wines he had tasted the world over, along with who had what stocks of the best vintages. How many pages had he filled with his meticulous handwriting? At best, the document would end up in some garbage can in the projects or the sewer.

Elisabeth would be here in a few hours, sitting on the edge of his bed. He would tell her everything. Well, what he could. The truth was, he couldn't remember much. It had all happened so quickly.

§ § §

"Yes, my love, the light had just turned green."

His wife would put a finger to his lips and said, "My poor darling, look at what they've done to you."

Sadness filled his face. He stared at her and said nothing more. Then he looked down. He was disappointed with himself. He had fallen into a trap and had not even put up a fight. He felt like a coward. She knew the words to reassure him and make him feel better. She told him that

5

she was thankful he was alive, that he should let the police do their job. Elisabeth then whispered a few sweet nothings. And they crossed their fingers and hoped for the best, as they always did when they faced life's hardships.

"They'll find your notebook, Benjamin. Don't worry. I'll call your editor."

"No, I'd prefer that you didn't. Don't tell anyone but Virgile."

Of course, Virgile Lanssien came with Elisabeth. He would not have left his employer's wife alone in such a crisis. Elisabeth went to find him in the hallway.

"Boss, how's it going? They really crushed you, didn't they?" Virgile teased, trying to lighten the mood when he saw the winemaker's bruised face.

Cooker smiled at the vineyard humor. His jaw hurt terribly, but he felt better with Elisabeth and Virgile at his side.

"I don't remember anything. Can you believe it? Nothing! Except that 1961 Latour. I wish you could have tasted it."

The nurse came in to change the bandages on Cooker's swollen face and caught Virgile's eye. He gave her a once-over, from neck to ankles, while Elisabeth hung up some clothes she had brought for her husband. Virgile winked at his boss.

"The snow has already melted," the young woman said, clearly sorry about that.

Cooker's eyes were half-closed. He winced when the nurse ran a damp cloth over his eyebrows to remove the dried blood.

"What handsome blue eyes you have, sir," she said, trying to divert his attention from what she was doing.

"I believe they are why my wife married me. Isn't that so, Elisabeth?"

"I won't argue with you today, not with what you've been through," Elisabeth said, kissing his hand.

Virgile seemed a little uncomfortable. He turned to the window. "I think it's going to snow again," he said to fill the silence.

The nurse looked at him and smiled with something less than innocence. To the impish grin she added, "From your lips to God's ear."

Virgile looked her in the eye and said, "If that were the case, the snowflakes would be angel feathers."

"You are a lucky man, Mr. Cooker, to have such a spiritual son," the nurse said.

§ § §

The week passed slowly, punctuated by bandage-changing sessions, lukewarm meals, temperature checks, and long periods of sleep. Christmas was a few days away. Large snowflakes were falling, as if covering the ground with a layer of protection. Carole was thrilled. The nurse had disclosed her first name to Cooker, perhaps in the hope that the information would get to Virgile.

"So he's not your son?"

"No, he's my assistant. He is very good at what he does."

Carole blushed and quickly changed the subject. "You are healing nicely. You were incredibly lucky. The man was that close to slitting your throat. If he had, you wouldn't have made it."

When she leaned over the bed, Cooker couldn't help staring at the three beauty marks on her chest. *This is ridiculous*, he thought, reproaching himself for his moodiness. *My face is not disfigured, it's just bruised.* He felt old, even though he was just fifty. Admittedly, the graying temples, a rebellious lock of hair, bushy eyebrows, and crow's-feet gave him a dignified charm. But was he still attractive? And why was he wondering this after having a narrow brush with death?

"Life is all about seduction," his father would have said. It was a maxim the man had practiced until his later years.

Still, Cooker was regaining some of his appetite for life, despite the anxiety attacks he suffered
in the middle of the night. He would wake up
in a sweat, pursued by hooded teenagers who
threw insults and lighters at him. Cooker knew
he would need time to process the trauma.

Carole, who clearly had a thing for Virgile,
was helping with her disarming innocence and
the childlike euphoria she expressed when she saw
snow on the rooftops.

"I hope it lasts until Christmas," she said con-
tinually, like a child repeating a prayer without
really believing in God or Santa Claus.

Cooker used whatever ploys he could to keep
her in his room. They would look out the window
and watch the snow swirl between the zinc rooftops and chimneys.

One afternoon, the winemaker loosened up
enough to tell her a personal story. He wasn't
positive it was true, but that didn't seem to matter.

"My father rarely left London, but one day be-
fore the war, he went off exploring southwestern
France. He ended up in Toulouse, visiting the
Basilica of Saint Sernin. He stayed at Le Grand
Balcon, the hotel where the famous aviators Jean
Mermoz and Antoine de Saint-Exupéry had met."

"I loved Saint-Exupéry's *The Little Prince*,"
Carole said, slipping her cross back and forth on
its chain.

9

"At the time, my father dreamed of being a pilot. He was only twenty. He stayed in Saint-Exupéry's room, where there was an old radio. He tried to tune into Radio London but got distracted by Radio Toulouse and the advertising slogan '*Dubo, Dubon, Dubonnet.*'"

The nurse laughed at Cooker's attempt to imitate the nasal tone of old-time radio hosts. He exaggerated it to please her.

"From his room, my father could see the Place du Capitole. Have you ever been to Toulouse?"

The nurse said no and mentioned her roots in Grenoble.

"The sky was gray, the weather uncertain, and Radio Toulouse announced, 'Dear listeners, direct from the Toulouse-Blagnac weather station, ninety-nine flakes of snow have fallen on our fine city, and the temperature is freezing. We are expecting more snow tomorrow, so get out your mittens. And now, Jean Sablon will sing '*Vous qui passez sans me voir.*'"

"Ninety-nine snowflakes. That was news in the day," Carole said.

"That's when my father said it was best to watch out for the French. He wrote his mother a letter to tell her about the ninety-nine snowflakes, and she told him to come home to London as soon as possible. She thought he was losing his mind. He even admitted to standing at his hotel window and counting snowflakes until dusk, coming up with far more than ninety-nine."

"I don't believe you," Carole said.

"It's true. I promise you it's true," Cooker answered in a deadpan voice. "My father did eventually get an explanation, something about how at the time, nobody improvised on the radio. They just read from notes. The radio announcer confused some shorthand for nine centimeters for ninety-nine snowflakes. He apparently got a good reprimand from his boss."

Cooker puffed up when the nurse laughed at his story, showing her flawless teeth. Then Virgile burst into the room. Carole turned around quickly, smoothed out her scrubs, and nearly knocked the winemaker's IV bag off the stand.

"Your torture is nearly over, Mr. Cooker. You should be getting out tomorrow."

Virgile watched the way Cooker and the nurse looked at each other as his assistant handed over the morning paper with a mischievous grin. The front-page story in the newspaper *France-Soir* caught the winemaker's eye immediately: "Grand Cru Heist. A hundred bottles of the famous 1989 Angélus premier grand cru classé were stolen last night from the renowned cellar at the Place de la Madeleine in Paris. The burglar stole only this internationally acclaimed Saint-Émilion and selected the very best vintage, which received top ranking in the *Cooker Guide.*"

Cooker pulled out the latest edition of his guide, which Virgile had brought him, and read his tasting notes in full.

"Who could want anything more for Christmas than some 1989 Angélus?" he asked.

Behind the attempt at humor, there was concern in his voice. He was thinking about his friend Hubert de Boüard de Laforest, who owned the premier grand cru mentioned in the article.

"How are you feeling today, sir?" Virgile asked.

"Like an ass who wasn't brave enough to fight and ended up in his shorts on the sidewalk." Cooker suddenly felt enraged. He tensed his jaw and pushed out his chest, as if he could not breathe. "They took everything, Virgile. Everything! All my notes. My entire guide. And my memories, my pride, my honor."

Virgile stared at his boss. Cooker pulled himself up on the bed and grimaced when he tried to turn to the window to hide the sob he felt coming on. Carole touched his shoulder.

"It's nothing, Mr. Cooker. Calm down. You'll be home tomorrow. You'll forget about it over time."

"And you've got all those notes in your head," Virgile added, also putting his hand on his boss's shoulder.

Just then, a cell phone rang.

"It's probably Elisabeth worrying about me," Cooker said. "Oh, it's you, darling? My little Margaux. I'm happy to hear your voice."

A smile came over his face. Virgile and Carole caught each other's eye and left Cooker, who was already looking more optimistic.

2

At the bottom of the valley, the Indre River flowed through patches of reverent willow trees. It was January, but it felt like an aging autumn in this part of the Touraine region. Lazy cows grazed in the pasture, just as they had in the summer. From the terrace of the Château de La Tortinière, Benjamin Cooker stared at the blurry lines of the landscape. In the distance, the Montbazon castle showed off its tower from another era. The Virgin Mary that rose above the edifice would have been demoralized by the ruins of the fortress. Recently, city workers had pulled off the ivy that had overgrown the fortifications, perhaps offering some redemption to the copper statue.

"Rest." Everyone—his doctors, of course, but also Elisabeth, Margaux, Virgile, and the others— kept saying the same thing. Sometimes Benjamin Cooker showed worrisome symptoms, with long silences that nobody dared to interrupt.

"This kind of attack is a violation, Mr. Cooker," a psychiatrist had told him in the hospital. "You will need weeks, perhaps even months to move on."

Cooker had closed his eyes. He was not convinced that Grangebelle, his retreat-like home in the Médoc, was the ideal spot for his convalescence. He needed new surroundings and new people.

He told Elisabeth and Virgile that he had chosen the Touraine because he still had a lot to learn about the wines in that region. He had visited the Loire River valley several times in the past. Vouvray, Bourgueil, and Chinon had pleased his palate, and he had often promised himself that he would explore this area further. It was known as France's garden, and the vineyards grew in the shadow of stone lacework castles. His stroke of bad luck had actually become an ideal pretext to wander the vineyards, even though they were bare at this time of year.

Cooker intended to stay until January 22, Saint Vincent's feast day. It was a symbolic choice. Saint Vincent was the patron saint of winegrowers, and with a little luck, the day would be "clear and beautiful" for "more wine than water," as the saying went. Elisabeth arrived with him and spent a few days, but she had to return to Grangebelle to take care of their dog,

Bacchus, who did not appreciate it when they were away too long.

"Can't you come home, Benjamin? I don't like the idea of leaving you alone. You're going to be bored in that hotel during the off season."

"Me, bored? With everything there is to see and drink? Don't worry, my love. I need to get my head together before I go home. If I set one foot in Grangebelle, I'd have to go to the office. I couldn't resist."

Aware that Elisabeth was not particularly re-assured, Cooker saw her off on the bullet train from Saint-Pierre-des-Corps to the Bordeaux-Saint-Jean station, where Alicia Santamaria, the Spanish immigrant who lived with Grangebelle's gardener, came to get her.

Elisabeth called her husband to say she had arrived safely and told him that Alicia had once again railed against France's lax immigration policies. Alicia blamed them for the country's rise in violent crime. In her mind, the assailants were probably North African.

"*Por Díos*, I can't believe what happened to monsieur!" Alicia had said, her Spanish accent tinged with Gascon. "They let everyone into France. *Qué misería*."

At Château de La Tortinière, Cooker knew he would find the solitude he needed to get over his fear of driving in cities and people asking him for

17

a light. But he didn't quite know how he would get through the weeks ahead of him.

He dropped into a rattan chair that beckoned in front of the balustrade. He wasn't feeling faint, but he did need to catch his breath. Cooker was about to ask for a glass of water but thought better of it. The concierge, Gaétan, was right there, looking concerned.

"It's nothing. I'd like a Bourgueil from the Domaine du Bel Air. Do you have some?"

He felt better when he saw Gaétan rush off, taking the stairs two at a time and then returning promptly. Cooker seemed to regain his sense of self before the wine glass was even full of the dark red liquid. He lifted the glass to his nose, while Gaétan, looking like a dignified Greek statue on a spacious estate, held the bottle, waiting for a verdict that would be brutally honest. The wine-maker sniffed aromas of berries and spices and picked up a few woody notes before bringing the glass to his lips. He savored the Bourgueil with the mannerisms of an experienced wine taster. He rolled the mouthful like a billiard ball on a pool table, lining his palate so as not to miss any of the full, round, ripe tannins in this excellent wine. From time to time, he clicked his tongue to refine his judgment. The concierge waited for the final decision. Cooker patted the chair next to him, beckoning the young man to sit down.

"I cannot enjoy this pleasure alone," Cooker said. Gaétan looked flattered by the invitation.

Cooker was the only guest at the hotel, so they could enjoy this luxury. La Tortinière would close for the season shortly, and the staff had been cut back.

Cooker shared his impressions of the wine. The concierge was hardly a novice and had a fairly refined palate himself. Cooker had found an ally, not unlike Virgile. Gaétan and Virgile were both about the same age, with expressive faces, a sense of humor, and a little clumsiness that made them charming.

Cooker and Gaétan chatted until the sun had disappeared behind La Tortinière's turrets. Cooker could no longer see Montbazon, and the cows had disappeared from the pasture as if by magic. The winemaker felt a chill and returned to his room. He would order dinner from room service before calling it a night. Tucked in his pocket was the hotel chef's recipe for saffron honey ice that Gaétan had gotten for him. Elisabeth would enjoy it.

Cooker went to sleep with Madame de Mortsauf. He had stopped at an antique book stand in the city of Tours and picked up a leather-bound copy of Honoré de Balzac's *The Lily of the Valley* that, curiously, had been used to dry flowers. Yellowed linden leaves and flower petals garnished every chapter, like exquisite bookmarks. The book gave off faded floral aromas, and Cooker devoured the novel. La Tortinière was his. He was alone in this manor that smelled of wax polish and holly. The owners lived in another building a hundred yards away.

"You're the master of the house," owner Anne Olivereau had said with a genuine charm that impressed the wine expert.

He had no bad dreams that night. Cooker was healing. The next day, he would get back to writing his guide. He had not told his editor what had happened and did not intend to. Saying nothing about it was a matter of pride.

§ § §

When Cooker woke up, he spotted a Morgan Plus 8 parked majestically in front of La Tortinière. It was deep green, very English, and gleamed on the white gravel. The winemaker smiled and left his room to admire the sports car. Such a jewel deserved respect. He was sure that its owner was a subject of Her Majesty the Queen.

The license plate proved Cooker correct. He caressed the chrome, as he would a sleeping tiger.

He walked around the car several times, peering in the windows to examine the convertible's interior.

A Morgan! He had dreamed of this car since he was a kid. The mechanics were way too fragile, but nothing could top it for luxury and elegance. Twenty years earlier, he had almost bought a very fine model that had belonged to French novelist André Malraux's son. But by the time he had convinced the bank to lend him the money, the beautiful English car had been snatched up by some fifteen-minute celebrity. The winemaker had never gotten over it and had fallen back on his Mercedes 280SL, which he now missed.

The concierge came to greet him and listened to Cooker expound on the car: how it could hold the road, the custom interior, the fine cylinders, and the specific sound its exhaust made. Gaétan was not particularly passionate about vintage cars but nevertheless asked a number of questions that Cooker was happy to answer. In exchange, Gaétan gave Cooker the name of the owner, a certain Sir Robert Morton, a middle-aged man accompanied by a gorgeous young blond woman who spoke "approximate" French and seemed to come from some Eastern Bloc country.

"They arrived at dawn, demanded a copious breakfast served with champagne—he wanted nothing but Moët—and asked not to be disturbed

under any circumstances," Gaétan said, lifting
an eyebrow.

The young man looked up at the lovers' room,
where the shutters were closed. Cooker imagined
the couple intertwined under wrinkled sheets.
Surely, it was some secret liaison that had found
refuge in this isolated hotel.

"I'll take my tea in the small dining room,"
Cooker said, rubbing his hands in anticipation of
meeting this Mr. Morton.

He was impatient to see the mysterious owner
of the Morgan and his conquest. He wolfed down
two croissants and drank three cups of tea. Then
the winemaker had to go see the car again. The
air was brisk, but the sight of the chrome reflecting the January sun revved Cooker's imagination.
With his British background, he would find the
right civilities and some common ground with
these people, who shared his passion. He was
already imagining himself riding through the
countryside behind the wheel of that convertible.
But the shutters remained hopelessly closed.

The concierge told Cooker about the pleasant
walks in the area, down by the river. He opted
for just a short walk around the hotel grounds,
which were covered with moss and ivy. A number
of trees watched over the La Tortinière manor.
Lebanese cedars, Japanese pagoda trees, sequoias,
and several varieties of evergreens formed a huge
nave that even bright sun had trouble penetrating.

The solitary walker tried to see the tops of each, but clearly the trees that surrounded the hotel were much older than the building.

The winemaker remembered what Gaétan had told him the evening before. La Tortinière's architect had been inspired by Charles Perrault's legendary *Sleeping Beauty*, even though the author had set his fairy tale in the Château d'Ussé, which was not far away. Cooker, however, refused to transform Mr. Morton into Prince Charming. He imagined him plump, slightly potbellied, wearing designer clothes. His Gold Card had to be the source of unimaginable charm, capable of seducing a Lolita who had managed to escape the streets of Budapest. But this Morton fellow did get the benefit of the doubt. He could not be completely lacking in taste if he drove a Morgan Plus 8.

Cooker walked deeper into the vegetation. Frozen leaves crackled under his shoes. A squirrel caught his attention and then took off on a path festooned with red berries. A slate-roofed farm appeared among the trees. Leading to it was an old drive lined with what looked like two-hundred-year-old holly bushes. Cooker was about to investigate when he heard steps behind him. He winced before recognizing a familiar voice. "Mr. Cooker, Mr. Cooker. There's a phone call for you."

Gaétan was out of breath, and his nose and cheeks were bright red from the cold. He asked Cooker to return to the hotel. The caller hadn't given his name, but he wanted to talk to the winemaker right away.

"It's urgent and personal," the young man said. "That's all that he told me."

Walking quickly, Cooker followed Gaétan but soon had to ask him to slow down because he couldn't keep up. When they arrived in front of the hotel, Cooker was disappointed to see that the Morgan was gone.

"Have Mr. Morton and his protégé already run off?" he asked.

"Rest assured, he's just gone to Tours in search of cigars, leaving his princess to sleep," Gaétan answered with a wink.

Cooker was liking this Morton more and more. Not only did he appreciate English cars and pretty women, but he also had an affinity for cigars. The man had to be an epicurean. With so much in common, they were destined to meet.

Cooker took the phone that sat on the marble reception desk.

"Hubert? What a surprise."

Cooker was happy to have his friend on the line. They hadn't spoken since some international tycoon had the gall to make an offer on his estate. Hubert had refused, of course. Château Angélus had been in the family for eight generations.

Hubert asked him how he was feeling. Yes, Cooker told him, he was feeling better. Yes, he was recovering his appetite for life. No, he had no news about his convertible, nor about his briefcase, but he still hoped to get his tasting notes back. They were of no interest to anyone but himself.

"But tell me, Hubert, what wouldn't you do to get people talking about your wine? I read in the paper that your Angélus is popular with thieves. Great publicity!"

Cooker noticed Gaétan listening discreetly as he arranged bottles of brandy on the shelves behind the bar. But he continued to speak loudly, as if he were alone in the hotel.

"It's a strange thing that happened. What is that you said?"

After every pause, the winemaker responded, "No! That's unbelievable."

Cooker saw that the concierge was even more curious about his mysterious half-sentences.

"It's a joke! Someone sent you a cryptic play on the Angélus devotion to the Virgin Mother—'Hail Hubert, full of grace. The Lord is with you, but your wine is not.' Whoever it is, he has a wicked sense of humor. I'm surprised he didn't send a bell, along with the card. It's too bad I only write guidebooks, because this would make a great novel, my friend."

The winemaker was now sitting in the golden leather armchair, as if to better enjoy the comical story his old friend Hubert de Boüard de Laforest was recounting.

But as Cooker continued to talk, he realized that Hubert didn't think that this was anything to joke about.

"Really, Hubert, it's just a prank. Why are you taking it so seriously?"

The two friends spoke for a long while, until an elegant figure made a noisy entrance in the château lobby. Cooker supposed it was the infamous Mr. Morton and gave him a slight nod while continuing the commentary on his friend's story. Then he cut the conversation short. "All you can do now is wait. If more of your wine is stolen, I suggest that you go talk to the police."

Cooker was still amused after he hung up. He had to share the story with someone. He would tell Gaétan, or maybe he would confide in the lanky Morton, who turned out to be as tall and dried up as a Tuscany yew tree. He was savoring a Cohiba and reading the *Herald Tribune.*

As soon as there was silence in the hotel lobby, the Englishman abandoned his reading and slipped his thin glasses into the inner pocket of his jacket. Then the owner of the Morgan got up and headed toward the clearly uninhibited guest whose telephone conversation had been all but public.

"*Excusez-moi*, sir, are you not Mr. Cooker, the well-known winemaker and critic?"

The man spoke broken French mixed with Oxford English. His diction was a little precious, as were his gestures. Cooker confirmed his identity with a smile and shook the Englishman's hand.

"Let me introduce myself. Robert Morton. I work in London for a wine brokerage."

"So, we share three passions," Cooker was quick to point out.

"I have no trouble imagining the first, but I must admit that I don't know what the two others could be, Mr. Cooker."

"From what I can tell, there are cigars, and are you not the happy owner of that dream car that's perfect for taking in Loire Valley's castles?"

Morton grinned. He rubbed his chin and asked the winemaker if he'd like a cup of tea. "Unless you would prefer coffee."

"With pleasure," Cooker said. "Thank you."

"A cigar?"

Robert Morton opened his shagreen case and took out a cigar with a band that Cooker recognized. He handed the Havana and the guillotine cutter to Cooker, whose friendship he seemed keen to nurture.

"So, Mr. Cooker, you like English beauties? I truly understand."

"Not always English, but I would go to Rocamadour on my knees for a Morgan."

"Where's that?" the Brit said.

The winemaker gave Morton a lesson in the history of that town in southwestern France that had attracted pilgrims for centuries. Smoke swirled above their heads, as the two men sized each other up. When Gaétan asked if they wanted more tea, they were speaking in English. There seemed to be no stopping them. Between two thick curls of smoke, they discussed New World wines, convertible sports cars, French and English rugby teams, Médoc wines, the cost of real estate in Périgord, southwestern French gastronomy, Charles de Gaulle, Churchill, Lady Diana, Charlotte Rampling, and Lord Byron, not to mention Cooker's recent misadventure in Paris.

Toward the middle of the day, the young woman who shared Morton's bed showed up, yawning. It looked like she had just climbed out of bed and thrown on a pair of jeans and a tight T-shirt. She was beautiful, tall, and had a lofty neck. With her full bust, she almost looked like a naïve and mischievous cherub—or a fallen angel whose steel-blue eyes said much about the pain they hid. Her elegant bone structure accentuated hollow cheeks and sensual lips.

"Did you sleep well, Oksana?" Morton asked in a flat voice.

Cooker was convinced that she meant little to this dandy, who pretended to know more about life than his age seemed to imply. For that matter, it took skill to guess the slender man's age. His flashy signet ring did, however, betray new money. That did not make the man any less likable. The new friends jumped at the idea of going to lunch at the Château d'Artigny. But the Morgan had only two seats. Oksana would be sacrificed on the altar of machismo.

"Go back to bed, darling. Tonight, we have a long drive. We have to be in Bordeaux before midnight." Robert Morton pecked her on the forehead.

Gaétan dried champagne glasses behind the bar and Cooker saw him looking her up and down. She pretended not to notice and walked out, swaying her hips in a way that was both seductive and rejecting.

3

Morton and Cooker finished off two bottles of
Vouvray. Their meal was copious, with a cori-
ander-flavored *nage de langoustines*, mullet filets
sautéed with endive, veal tenderloin with morels,
and a slow-cooked carrot and orange dessert.
Then Artigny's sommelier dug up some aged rum
that called for two cigars—double coronas from
Partagas. After everything he had been through in
Paris, nothing was more important to Benjamin
Cooker's morale than savoring the present.

The two men were in brilliant form and raised
their glasses to life, love, and their respective
success. By the time Morgan revved up his sweet
engine to drive back to La Tortinière, neither of
the two men could even pretend to be lucid. The
aged rum from Martinique had definitely cheered
them up, and the road from the restaurant back
to the hotel seemed to have quite a few more
bends and curves than it did earlier in the day.
Even the chill in the air was not enough to nip

their euphoria. A frowning Gaétan met the two staggering men in front of the hotel.

"Did you have a fine lunch, sirs?" he asked and then stammered, "Um, Mr. Morton, the young woman accompanying you preferred to call a taxi and asked me to tell you not to try to contact her. Uh, that's what she said."

The Englishman swore under his breath. Cooker looked down and said, "I'm terribly sorry. It's my fault."

"Not at all, Benjamin. It's perhaps the best thing that has happened to me today."

"If you say so," Cooker said, looking doubtful.

"Gaétan, a double rum, please."

"Right away, sir," the concierge responded. "And for you, Mr. Cooker?"

"The same," the winemaker said, keen on not abandoning his partner in crime.

Robert Morton collapsed in an armchair. It swallowed him up. His bony knees and the wounded-bird expression on his face were all that Cooker could see. Morton emptied his glass in one gulp and asked for his hotel bill. This bothered Cooker. Morton was evidently more concerned than he had said. The winemaker tried to dissuade him from driving in his state, but in vain. The Englishman insisted that he could not be late for his appointment in Bordeaux and waved a weak good-bye.

"Business, my dear Cooker. You know what our line of work requires."

Cooker nodded. He finished his rum, and, from La Tortinière's front steps, watched Morton zoom down the drive in his vintage Morgan. *Well, that was a short-lived friendship,* he thought. Not wanting to be alone, he headed to the bar and ordered another rum from Gaétan, who said nothing.

Mr. Morton was a strange man. *This* Cooker knew. Otherwise, he knew very little about him, although he was sure their paths would cross again. He intuited it as he examined the bottom of his glass, like a fortune-teller reading tea leaves. Alas, the hotel's rum was more rustic than the one at Château d'Artigny, and Cooker did not finish his glass. He huddled in a chair for a long time, missing Morton already. He would have liked to see Oksana in her tight jeans again, and he would have loved driving that Morgan, even just around the grounds or on a short trip to Montbazon. *Had it all been a dream?* The rum was making him doubt the very existence of the eccentric and enigmatic Morton.

He ended up falling asleep in the armchair. The crackling of wood and the pungent aroma of smoking vine shoots awakened him a short time later. Gaétan had lit a fire. Cooker apologized to the concierge, as if he had been caught red-handed being lazy.

"Would you like to have dinner in your room tonight, Mr. Cooker?" Not giving the winemaker a chance to gather his thoughts, Gaétan added, "I can make you a truffle omelet, if you'd like."

"Nothing," Cooker said dryly.

Then, changing his mind, he added, "Please, bring me a glass of water and two antacid tablets."

Gaétan made a teasing face and removed the glass of rum from the table. Cooker pulled himself out of the armchair and walked over to the fireplace. Heat was beginning to spread throughout the dark lounge. He thought about Grangebelle and Elisabeth, who was alone in that large house with nobody but Bacchus. At this hour, they would be able to see strands of light from the Blaye power station rippling on the silt-laden waters of the Gironde.

§ § §

Cooker couldn't sleep that night and took a sedative. When he woke up, a young waiter who looked nothing like Gaétan brought a tray into his room at the promised time: Grand Yunnan tea, bread with butter and apricot jam, just the way he had it at Grangebelle. The famous winemaker was not a man to change his habits. He had asked that they find him an English-language paper, *The Herald Tribune* if possible, but there was only the French daily, *Le Figaro*, on the tray. The teenager apologized, as if he had made a serious mistake. Cooker stopped himself from snarling and said, "It's not important."

He then informed the boy that his shirt was buttoned wrong. The boy looked down, horrified, and apologized again, "Don't hold it against me, sir. I had to replace Gaétan at the last minute. Nobody knows where he is."

Cooker started questioning the replacement, who turned out to be the owners' nephew.

"Perhaps he's sick and can't answer the phone?"

"I don't know, sir. We knocked on his door, but nobody answered. Mrs. Olivereau said he never sleeps anywhere else."

Cooker, who was both surprised and impatient to find out more, plopped his toast back on the plate.

The boy looked like he had said too much and asked to be excused. Cooker pulled a ten-euro bill out of his pocket and handed it to the teenager. Then he stood silently in front of his window. He heard the door close behind him and tried to focus on the distant statue of the Virgin Mary. A layer of milky fog covered her from head to toe. Cooker put on his glasses, as if it would help him glimpse the Madonna's thin smile.

It was nearly eleven in the morning when he finally decided to leave his room. Reading *Le Figaro* was not enough to remedy the disagreeable sensation of being hung over. He wasn't nauseous, but he was definitely grumpy.

When he started down the stairs, he was surprised by all the activity in the lobby. Four local police officers were questioning the hotel owner, who appeared to be saddened by what she was hearing.

"Yes, that's her," Mrs. Olivereau said, pointing at the dog-eared picture the officer showed her.

A young cop was jotting down everything that his superior officer said. He was squeezed into a uniform that was too tight, and his face reddened when the officer started talking faster.

"You say she arrived with a certain Mr. Morton yesterday morning? What was he like? Can you describe him?"

Cooker stopped on the stairs, his hand on the rail. He held his breath, not wanting to miss a word of the conversation.

"Can we see the couple's room?" the detective asked, sounding somewhat satisfied with the way things were going.

"The room was cleaned immediately after Mr. Morton's departure. I fear you won't find anything there," said the château owner, who now seemed very distraught.

"It's a formality," the captain said without looking at her.

As he stood on the stairs, Cooker knew the investigators would eventually notice him, and they did. It was hard to tell if they looked at him with scorn or suspicion. They turned back to the reception desk, as if it were the hotel owner's responsibility to announce the identity of this very distinguished guest, who was wearing an impeccable suit but still seemed a bit disheveled from the night before.

"Ah, Mr. Cooker. Did you sleep well?"

"To be honest, not at all."

"I'm so sorry to hear that," the owner said. She then explained the presence of the police with a short sentence. "These men are here to ask some questions about the young woman who was here with Mr. Morton yesterday."

"Oksana?" Cooker asked.

"Do you know her?" the captain asked.

"I would have liked to know her better, if you see what I mean," he said with a mischievous smile, trying to cover his sudden concern that something had happened to her.

"What was her name again?"

"Oksana. That is how she was introduced to me. I didn't ask to see her ID. I'm pretty sure that she was not French. Isn't that so?"

"You are right," the captain answered. "She was born in Minsk."

Cooker slipped his hands into the pockets of his flannel pants. "I'm not all that sure she was over eighteen," he said.

"Nothing escapes you, does it, Mr., um, what was your name again?"

"Cooker. Benjamin Cooker," he said, handing his card to the captain, who looked suitably impressed.

"You look familiar. Have I seen you on television?"

"I rather doubt that," Cooker said.

The young officer who was taking notes looked at Cooker with wide eyes. The winemaker suspected that he wasn't used to seeing people standing up to his boss.

"Mr. Cooker, what do you know about Robert Morton? I believe you had lunch with him yesterday."

"Nothing. I know nothing," Cooker said before adding, "That is, nothing I have had time to verify. I can only tell you about his car and his supposed business as a wine broker. I could tell you everything about his Morgan but zilch about him."

The telephone at the reception desk rang. The hotel owner grabbed it.

"It's for you, Mr. Cooker. It's Chief of Police Fourquet from Paris."

"Please excuse me," Cooker said, slipping between the officers to take the phone.

"Yes, Chief. Some good news?"

The lead local officer at the reception desk was obviously hanging onto every word Cooker said and seemed irritated by how easily the winemaker took charge.

"Where is that you say? In Leipzig?"

Cooker's face suddenly lit up.

"What state is it in? Good, good. How did you find it? Aha! German intuition, perspicacity and rigor! I never understood how they lost the war." Cooker laughed.

"What's my new license plate again—1955 JO 6I, you said? I didn't know all the subtleties. Do I owe you a Château Latour? A 1961, of course. That was a fantastic year. No, really, it's my pleasure. It won't be at La Tour d'Argent, though. Too many bad memories."

Had Cooker been in the same room with Chief Fourquet, he would have kissed him on both cheeks. After thanking him again, he hung up the phone, looking thrilled.

"Captain, if you stopped a navy-blue Mercedes with a French license plate reading 1955 JO 6I and found an Albanian wearing an Orthodox cross and sunglasses behind the wheel, what would you do?"

The captain stared at him. He didn't seem to appreciate how familiar Cooker was being with him. *He probably considers me insolent,* Cooker thought.

"Uh, I would check his identity and his driver's license."

"Wrong answer, Captain! Europe does not have any borders anymore, and you should know, my friend, that the car was stolen, and the plates were faked by someone who did not know that the letters 'O' and 'I' have been banished from European plates."

The captain blushed. Cooker grinned.

"Champagne, Mrs. Olivereau! Champagne for everyone. My car was just found in Germany. Which, for a Mercedes, you must admit, is not out of the ordinary."

The waiter from breakfast was lining up the champagne flutes on the counter. Cooker summarized his recent experience in Paris. The winemaker's relaxed approach seemed to have an effect on the foursome of local police, and they took off their caps and sipped a little champagne.

Cooker went on to praise the hotel and its owners, along with the staff that was so attentive to detail and able to react so quickly. But he added that he had hoped to see Gaétan. That is when Cooker, realizing he still had questions about Oksana, asked the captain why he was inquiring about her.

"I'm sorry, Mr. Cooker. She's dead," the captain replied. "A jogger found her body this morning on the banks of the Loire."

Cooker frowned as the captain explained that the prostitute from Minsk, who was barely seventeen years old, had been strangled with copper wire, which was also found on the riverbank. It didn't appear that she had fought back. She still had her clothes on, and they weren't dirty or torn. She wasn't wearing any jewelry. The only thing she had with her was a card from the Château de La Tortinière. It was in the back pocket of her jeans. Scribbled on it was a cell phone number.

Nobody at the hotel, not even Cooker, had spent any time with her. Morton had treated her like some kind of plaything that he wanted to keep all to himself.

"The only person who could perhaps tell you anything, Captain, is Gaétan, our concierge, but he didn't show up for work today," Mrs. Olivereau said, obviously not in the mood for the Deutz, whose fine bubbles were quite out of place, considering the circumstances. It was clear to Cooker that nobody felt like celebrating.

"It's not like him," Mrs. Olivereau said. "He's a real asset here, and he's always available."

"Did you try to call him at home?" the captain asked, setting down his glass as well.

"He lives on the grounds, but he didn't answer his door when we knocked. We finally opened it with our own passkey. He wasn't there."

"Doesn't he have a cell phone?"

"We thought of that, but it just goes to voice mail."

Cooker, who had listened without saying anything, set his champagne flute on the fireplace mantel and turned to the hotel owner. "Would you mind giving us his cell phone number?"

"Of course, Mr. Cooker."

Mrs. Olivereau wrote down her employee's number on a piece of paper. She held it out to the winemaker, who approached the captain.

"Would you mind comparing this number with the one you found in Oksana's pocket?"

The captain scowled but followed Cooker's suggestion.

The silence that followed confirmed Cooker's hunch. The atmosphere in the room grew heavy. The hotel owner could not believe that Gaétan, her loyal employee, could possibly be involved in such a sordid affair. Not him! It was not possible.

"You don't think that...?" Mrs. Olivereau stammered.

The winemaker let the captain answer.

"I'll have to put out an APB immediately. You must admit, ma'am, that the disappearance of your concierge does coincide with the young girl's murder."

"Yes, I understand," the hotel owner said, clearly reluctant to admit the obvious.

The bottle of Deutz stood in the bucket of ice, and nobody even considered pouring more. The four cops had put their hats back on. La Tortinière was in a state of shock. Even Benjamin Cooker could not imagine the young man he had just met was a murderer. This quiet retreat on the banks of the Indre wasn't turning out to be so restful.

4

A day had not gone by without a phone call from Virgile. Cooker suspected that it was a feeling of helplessness, rather than thoughtfulness, prompting his assistant's calls. He sensed Virgile worried that the convalescence would drag on and that he couldn't carry on all by himself. After all, Cooker was overly sensitive, as much as he tried to hide it behind an easy-going attitude or the opposite, a foul temper. He was also impulsive and never went half way. This supposed retreat in the country, which he had decided on without really consulting Virgile, would inevitably have some repercussions.

And to be quite frank, rest and relaxation were not Cooker's strong points. The sooner he got back to his office on the Allées de Tourny in Bordeaux, the sooner he would return to his usual witty, strong-minded self. Furthermore, over the past two weeks, samples had been piling up in the lab, and a number of his loyal customers had been trying to get in touch with him. He was being summoned not only to South Africa and Argentina but also to Burgundy and near Rasteau in Provence, where, according to his lab tech Alexandrine de la Palussière, there were a few pending emergencies. Without Cooker, day-to-day business was turning into a mess.

"Sir, you're wanted all over the place."

"That's giving me too much credit. For now, I'm doing a Vouvray cure. Once I've gotten through it, perhaps, my dear Virgile, I will focus on the small concerns of Cooker & Co. As for Rasteau, you should go, my good man. And give me a report."

Before hanging up, Cooker added, "By the way, Virgile, from now on, you are forbidden to say anything bad about the police. This morning, I learned that they found my convertible. It got picked up in Leipzig!"

"Where's that?"

"In Germany."

"You can't expect me to know the names of twenty-five hundred grape varieties and also be skilled in geography," Virgile said, clearly pleased with the news.

"I agree, but you could improve very quickly by taking the first plane to Berlin and bringing my favorite toy home, if you see what I mean."

"Which implies that I swing by the Loire Valley to pick you up, I gather."

"You're a quick learner. Go strut your stuff across the Rhine."

"What about Rasteau?"

"Rasteau can wait. They are as close to paradise as you can get. Nature serves them well. Isn't patience the mother of all virtues? Use that as an excuse when you talk to the head of the coop. He's a friend of mine, another one of those winemakers who left Bordeaux, selling his soul to the devil in Provence."

Virgile laughed. He seemed to be pleased with the turn of events and the tone of the conversation. "I'll be at La Potinière in under two days."

"It's Tortinière, Virgile. Clean your ears, for God's sake."

"And what about your notebook? Still no news?"

"Don't even mention it."

Changing the subject, Cooker asked, "Anything new in Bordeaux?"

"Yes, in fact, the shop La Vinothèque de Dionysos on Cours de l'Intendance was robbed last night. It was weird. Just like in Paris, they took only the Angélus."

"I'm surprised my friend Hubert de Boüard has not called me yet. How many bottles?"

"I don't know, but it's your friend Mr. Delfranc, the former cop from Saint-Estèphe, who called the office to tell you. He asked after you and wants you to call him when you have a chance."

"Nothing else?"

"Oh, yes. Someone broke into Alexandrine de la Palussière's apartment."

"What did they take?"

"Nothing. That's what's strange about it."

"It's not a thief, then, but one of her exes," Cooker said, sure of himself.

"That's going a bit far, sir."

"Women are ghastly to each other, my dear Virgile. You're too young to know that."

"Excuse me for being so naïve."

"I'm not interested in Ms. de la Palussière's private life. But before you get your ticket for Germany, go sniff around La Vinothèque de Dionysos. I want to know which vintages were stolen, how many bottles, and, for that matter, how the thieves pulled off the heist."

"Fine, Mr. Cooker," Virgile said, sounding excited.

"Perfect. I'll let the authorities in Leipzig know that you are coming, and before you leave, send Alexandrine some flowers from me."

"Roses?"

"Whatever you like. After all, you're the one who knows how to communicate with women."

Cooker cut the conversation short when the hotel owner told him a certain Hubert de Boüard was on one of the hotel's lines.

"I'll take it right away," he said.

An impish look was returning to his eyes.

"Hello, Hubert? I need to give you my cell phone number again so you don't have to keep calling the front desk. I just heard the news from Virgile. You've devised a very clever publicity campaign, my friend. Your wine will be all over the papers tomorrow."

"Oh... Why do you say that?" The man from Saint-Émilion spoke in a hushed tone, his anxiety seeping through. "Benjamin, I got another one of those messages in the mail today."

"A message?" Cooker asked, just a bit impatient. "Explain yourself."

"This morning, I got another card. It was the same as the other day. But this one said, 'Your Angélus is gone, and you don't stand a prayer.' And after that, well—"

"And after that, what?"

"It said, 'Two from you.'"

"Nothing else?"

"Nothing."

"Where was it sent from?"

"Spain. Madrid to be exact."

Cooker paused. "Two from you? This has to be connected to the heist that took place last night at La Vinothèque de Dionysos in Bordeaux. I can't say that I'm happy to be the one to break the news."

"This is unbelievable," Hubert de Boüard said.

"As was the case with the Place de la Madeleine in Paris, the thieves took only your Angélus. I bet the investigators are going to think you're behind this. I hope you have a good lawyer."

"But, Benjamin..."

"I'm not kidding. This is very curious. Do you have any enemies? Be honest with me, Hubert."

"I swear, Benjamin, I don't understand this at all. I just hope it's some kind of prank, a practical joke."

"This could very well be a practical joke, Hubert. There's no reason to panic. Let's just wait and see."

Cooker promised the Angélus estate owner that he would stop by as soon as he was back in Bordeaux, perhaps as early as the following week.

"What about you, Benjamin? How are you feeling after what happened?"

"Helping out friends like you is restoring my appetite for life. You wouldn't believe it, but one of the guests at the hotel where I'm supposed to be resting was found murdered on the banks of the Loire, and the concierge has inexplicably disappeared. It's alarming, isn't it?"

"My mysterious cards must seem dull in comparison."

"Don't be so sure. I wouldn't let anyone sully the image of Angélus. You know how highly I regard your wine. Actually, I think it's polite of your robbers to inform you every time they commit a break-in. And, as far as I know, they take only the best years. Connoisseurs. You should be happy, Hubert, at the quality of the people who are getting your fine wines into the news."

"Is that how you see it?"

"Frankly, you would be wrong to think of them any other way," Cooker said.

"Perhaps you are right," the Château Angélus owner said, still a little bit skeptical. "Do you think I should tell the police?"

"Wait for the next card. That way you'll have ample evidence, and you can minimize the possibility of being treated badly by some dismissive rules-obsessed detective."

"Before this is all over, I might be saying a few extra prayers myself—I don't care what the card said."

"I see you have recovered your sense of humor. Sleep soundly, Mr. de Boüard."

The winter sun had barely won the duel it had been fighting since the early hours of the day with the layers of fog spread over the Indre. Now its pale rays were sparkling on the lazy river. The winemaker felt like walking to escape the grim atmosphere in the château. He was starting to really miss the Médoc. And he could not get his mind off the Angélus case.

Cooker was used to taking long walks in the vineyards and pine groves in the company of his impertinent dog, Bacchus, but he had underestimated the distance that separated La Tortinière from the banks of the Indre. The path he took—it was the one the concierge had liked so much—ran through the woods, the moor, and pastures where cows grazed nonchalantly. He had dressed warmly and had picked up a hazel tree branch to use as a walking stick, as well as a weapon. Since his attack, he was always on guard. He turned to the right and followed a wall bordering a battalion of poplar trees filled with noisy birds. Otherwise, everything seemed peaceful. Cooker sat down on a worm-eaten fallen tree trunk between two weeping willows whose flimsy branches dipped into the slack waters of the river.

The church bells in Montbazon rang out at noon. Cooker was getting hungry, and his stomach was beginning to growl. High up on the top of the hill, La Tortinière was nothing more than a rock formation surrounded by a luxuriant English garden. Gray wisps of smoke were floating out of the chimneys. The winemaker followed them until they melded with the clouds. A sudden desire to eat roasted perch renewed his energy, and he decided to cut across the fields. He was a little winded and trying not to slip on the wet ground when he saw a tall form under a gnarled apple tree.

Wearing dark pants and a white shirt spattered with mud, Gaétan was staring straight ahead, a hemp rope tight around his neck. There was a surprised look on his bluish, nearly purple face. His mouth was open, and his swollen black tongue was hanging out. At the foot of the tree, the winemaker noticed footprints, as if the boy had hesitated at length before putting an end to his life.

5

I didn't think I would see you again so soon," the police captain said, sounding almost pleased when he saw Cooker holding his hands in front of the fireplace to warm them.

"We are going to end up being regular fixtures here at La Tortinière," Cooker said, trying to sound friendly.

"I would gladly have skipped that honor considering the circumstances," the captain responded. "I must say, though, the investigation is moving along."

"Is it?"

"It's all clear now. Don't you think, Mr. Wine Expert?"

Cooker figured the detective wasn't going to let him get the upper hand again.

"Not really. I think it's an even bigger mystery."

"How is that?"

"For now, nothing proves that Gaétan murdered the girl."

"Yet you are the one who clued us in."

"I know, but we need, oh, sorry, *you* need more solid evidence."

"Remorse, Mr. Cooker. Remorse. Perhaps there was no premeditation to get rid of the girl. But you know, this is a classic case. A prostitute refuses to submit. They have words. There's the excitement, the violence, the rape perhaps, and in the heat of the moment, the irreparable. Then his conscience takes over, and he doesn't want to be judged by others. He is horrified by what he has done and needs to pay the price."

"If I may toss a little sand into this well-oiled machine, Captain. Do we know if the killer took advantage of his victim?"

"The girl's autopsy results won't be in for another hour, but it is highly likely."

"Haste makes waste, Captain."

"I'll grant you that."

"I presume you will order an autopsy on the concierge."

"Of course, that's procedure, even though it is a fairly obvious suicide."

"I recommend that you visit the site where he was found. The view of the Indre is very picturesque."

Cooker spoke without too much sarcasm. This police captain was friendlier now than he was the first time they had met. "Didn't you notice the mud on his clothes and the scratches on his arms?"

The captain did not give Cooker the opportunity to continue his argument. "It's likely that the girl tried to fight him off. Maybe she even bit him."

"If I remember correctly, there was no sign of a struggle. At any rate, you'll compare the DNA, I suppose."

"You're not trying to tell me how to do my job, are you?" the captain asked, smiling.

"That is not at all my intention."

"In any case, although the two deaths are most certainly related in some way, the first scenario might not be the right one."

"The only connection between the concierge and the girl is the concierge's phone number," Cooker said.

"Now that we're on that, I'm wondering if it was his handwriting," the captain said.

"You didn't check?" Cooker asked.

"You're being a nuisance, for God's sake. Do I ask you if the wine you make is watered down, or if you take kickbacks from certain estates listed in your damned guide?"

The winemaker did not bat an eye. He stood up calmly and headed toward the armchair, where he had left his jacket. He took out a small notebook and scribbled a few notes in pencil. The detective watched without saying a word.

As Cooker wrote, the flashing blue and red lights of the police cruisers and ambulance began sweeping the walls of the lounge. Cooker heard heavy footsteps and dull voices. He went out to the front to watch the ambulance leave, taking Gaétan's body to the morgue in Tours. Cooker remembered the question that Gaétan had asked him not that many hours earlier. The naïveté had moved him: "Tell me, Mr. Cooker, how do you become France's most famous winemaker?"

"You know, Gaétan, I am just an amateur, but I don't settle for anything less than the best. The rest is just luck."

"Luck?"

"Yes, luck," Cooker had said.

Fatigued and demoralized, Cooker returned to the hotel lounge. The captain had vanished. The hotel staff, meanwhile, had red eyes and long faces. The winemaker went to his room to rest, but he could not find sleep. Virgile would arrive the next day, before this tragic story could be cleared up. The girl's murder had shocked Cooker. She had seemed so vulnerable. And what part had Gaétan played in all of this? He had been such a conscientious hotel employee.

There was a knock at the door. Two shy knocks.

"Leave me alone," Cooker grumbled.

"It's Captain Guilhem."

Cooker got off the bed and opened the door.

"By all means, come in."

"I wanted to apologize for earlier."

"No harm done."

"I should hope not," the captain said.

"Let's say the case is closed. I wasn't too polite to you either. What would you like to drink, Captain?"

"No alcohol. My day's not finished yet."

Cooker opened the minibar tucked inside a sturdy wood cupboard. He set two cans of orange juice on the table he used for writing. "With or without ice?"

"Never any ice," the captain said, having recovered some of his self-assurance.

"You're right. I hate ice myself."

"I was right! You're not the kind to put water in your wine," the captain said, setting his cap on the bed.

"Too bad I'll be leaving tomorrow, as I think the two of us could have gotten along," Cooker added, sloughing off his grumpy attitude.

"Your contribution would, in fact, always be welcome."

"Consider it yours, Captain."

"You will return to your wine, and the day after tomorrow, you will have forgotten the misadventures that occurred at La Tortinière."

"So you call a double murder a misadventure?"

"You don't believe Gaétan's death was suicide?"

"Not any more than I believe Oksana was raped," Cooker said.

"Yes, we did get the autopsy results after you went upstairs: there was no sign of sexual abuse, but hairs found on the girl belonged to the concierge."

"Do you have the hotel business card that you found in the girl's pocket?" Cooker asked.

"Yes."

"Would it be possible to see it?"

"Of course."

The winemaker took the card and went over to the bedside table, which was piled with wine-related publications and a few glossy wine-auction catalogs. Gaétan's recipe for the saffron honey ice cream was sticking out of one of the magazines. Cooker compared the writing against what was on the card.

"It's an ice cream recipe," the winemaker told the captain. "Gaétan was kind enough to ask the chef for it."

"And?"

"See for yourself, Captain. There are enough numbers in the list of ingredients to prove that it was not the concierge who wrote down his phone number on that business card."

"That doesn't change anything," the captain said.

"True. One could also imagine that she gave herself to the boy and then wrote down his number."

"How poetic, Mr. Cooker. I myself am prag-matic. That is certainly why we are not in the same line of work."

"In the name of that pragmatism, you should know that in prostitution, the john reveals more of himself than the woman who pretends to be enjoying it."

"Mr. Cooker, you seem to have experience in this area that I, alas, cannot claim."

"Now, now, it's human nature. You're a bit of a prude, Captain. Yet the card was found in Oksana's jeans and not in his."

"I'll give you that. If she didn't write it down, and neither did her friend, or lover, or customer, whatever you want to call him, then who did?"

"Quite simply, someone who wanted to point the finger at him," Cooker said.

"You are Machiavellian, Cooker."

"No, just pragmatic," Cooker said, smiling.

The captain studied the woodwork while he finished his orange juice, making a face with his last swig. Then there was a knock on the door.

"What do you know. I should open an office here," Cooker said. "Come in."

A deputy came into the room. He approached his superior officer and whispered a few words in his ear. The two men then stared at Cooker's shoes.

"Would you like to know where I get my Lobbs?" the winemaker asked without a trace of sarcasm. "I don't want to disappoint you, but they are not Berluttis."

"Excuse me?" the captain said, "I believe this is more criminal than it is political." After chuckling, he added, as if to polish off his adversary, "Pardon my nosiness, Mr. Cooker, but could you please tell me what size you wear in—what was it now—Lobbs?"

"Well, what a fine idea! Forty-two and a half, European size. I'm partial to that half. At my age, even a demi-measure matters. I see that you have finally decided to analyze the footprints under the apple tree, which I thought were suspicious from the start."

The captain interrupted him. "Roussin, you can speak freely in front of the gentleman. We are beginning to share the same views on this strange case. I get the feeling this is not our last surprise."

"We found size forty-one, which corresponds with the concierge's shoes, and a few between size forty-two and forty-three. I suppose those are yours, Mr. Cooker?"

The winemaker did not answer.

"We also found size forty-five footprints. Actually, they were closer to forty-six. They led down to the river. That's a lot of people for one dead man," the captain said, sighing and rubbing his neck.

"I'm pleased to see you're coming around to my point of view, Captain. If you aren't susceptible to heartburn, you deserve a second orange juice."

"You are very kind, Mr. Cooker, but one should never overdo a good thing."

"Really? I will not insist. I admire your restraint."

6

To celebrate Virgile's arrival, Benjamin Cooker uncorked a bottle of Bonnezeaux from the Petits-Quarts estate, a 1997 Le Malabé. The honey-colored wine was just as sweet as it should be, full of fruit and flowers. It was the perfect accompaniment to convivial conversation. Virgile admitted that he knew nothing about this wine, which came from three small shale hills overlooking the village of Thouarcé.

Cooker just had to slip outside, his glass in hand, to admire his car. The convertible had not suffered during its absence. It was as shiny as it had been the day he bought it. There was just a little scratch on the right side.

"I had to show my credentials to get the keys, and I almost came back empty-handed," Virgile recounted, clearly satisfied with having brought his boss's wheels back.

"The Germans are a bit persnickety, to say the least," Cooker said, still delighting in his car.

"Worse than that, I'd say, more like pains in the ass."

"A true German can't stand the French, but he gladly drinks their wines. I'm not the first person to say this. I'm quoting a German writer. Who do you think it is?"

"Um, I'd say Goethe," the assistant guessed, looking a little embarrassed.

"Congratulations, Virgile. You always surprise me."

"I don't deserve any praise. He's the only German writer I know. By the way, you have forty-eight hours to change the license plates, or else you'll have more problems on your hands. There's a special permit from the Leipzig police in the glove compartment."

"It'll be done tomorrow," Cooker said.

"So we're not hitting the road tonight?" Virgile asked.

"I wouldn't ask that of you, considering all the miles you've just driven."

"I don't feel tired at all."

"But I do," Cooker said firmly.

"You're still recuperating, sir."

"True, but that isn't the only thing that's been on my mind," the winemaker said, knitting his bushy eyebrows. "Strange things have been happening here."

"What kind of strange things?"

"Two crimes in under twenty-four hours."

"And that's all?" Virgile said, whistling. "Yes, strange things, as you say."

"And I haven't told you the half of it."

"Well you have either told me too much or too little. Two crimes—that's something."

"I agree."

The wrinkles on Cooker's forehead deepened, making him look even more pensive, and then he added, "The Bonnezeaux awaits us. We don't want it to get too warm."

"In the meantime, you're teasing me. What's the weapon? Who are the victims? Is there a motive?"

"To tell you the truth, I haven't the slightest idea."

"That doesn't seem like you."

"And yet that's the way it is. But this is not a conversation to have without a drink. Quick, let's go in."

They stopped at the reception desk, and Cooker reserved a room for his assistant. Then they found a small lounge where they could discuss Oksana's murder and Gaétan's supposed suicide. Virgile listened attentively. He looked perplexed. Then he said, "I really like the aromas of ripe, almost candied fruit, the citrus and exotic fruit, along with a hint of toasted…"

Cooker was surprised. This was not what he expected to hear from Virgile. Then he thought better of it and followed his assistant's lead. "I wonder if I don't prefer the following year. It's in the same range, with flattering aromas, concentrated flavor, and a fine finale. It is very representative of the appellation—both intense and light, refined and flowery, without being diluted. It is always refreshing but with a kind of warmth. Bonnezeaux is a sure bet, like the Coteaux du Layon, and they age well. One day, we will come back to explore the Anjou wines under circumstances that are, well, calmer. I am sure you'll like it here."

"You are in brilliant form, Mr. Cooker! I'm happy to see you like this, after what you have been through. But I still don't know if you invited me to the Loire Valley to get your car back or to help you unravel this strange case of an Eastern European whore who was bumped off for who-knows-what reason."

"You wouldn't talk like that if you had met Oksana."

"Which means?"

"The Virgile I know would have been all over her in a minute and not too long thereafter in her bed."

"No, that is for other men. For an inexperienced concierge, perhaps, or a lonely hotel guest suffering from midlife lust. That's not my style. You understand, don't you?"

"Not exactly," Cooker said, clearly goading Virgile.

"I never was very good at drawing pictures."

"Then I'll let you off the hook. But follow through on your thoughts. I'm interested."

Cooker had picked up the bottle of wine and was preparing to fill Virgile's glass. The young man stopped him.

"I'm no cop, but I'd bet a case of your Bonnezeaux that this has something to do with Morton, the Morgan Man."

"What makes you so sure of yourself?"

Cooker was not ready to accept this suggestion. Robert Morton, the refined and cultivated dandy who had been his well-mannered compatriot for a day, had to be an honest man. He would bet on it. He was prepared to stand up for Morton's integrity. Except that he knew absolutely nothing about this person, who said he worked in wines but had no business card to show for it.

"He said he had to leave right away for an important meeting in Bordeaux," Cooker said without much conviction.

"In Bordeaux. Well, well."

"There's nothing unusual about that for an international wine broker."

"If you say so," Virgile said. "Then we just might run into him. You can't cross the Aquitaine Bridge in a Morgan Plus 8 without being noticed. So, sir, tell me, do you know a lot of English brokers who drive across France in that kind of convertible, when vintage car collectors are hard pressed to take that kind of car out of the garage once a year?"

The winemaker did not like the young man's tone, but he had to admit he had no arguments to counter Virgile's line of reasoning. With his innocent air, Virgile had once again found faults in a pristine picture.

§ § §

For the first time since he had arrived in the Touraine region, Cooker had no trouble falling asleep. Calm had returned to La Tortinière. They departed at the first light of dawn. Cooker left a thank-you note at the reception desk while Virgile put their bags in the car. Then the winemaker slipped into the beige driver's seat. He rubbed the leather-covered steering wheel and the walnut dashboard. Then he adjusted the rearview mirror. Finally, he turned the key and revved the engine. Virgile was already asleep by the time they got onto the A10 highway.

Cooker turned the radio down low, so as not to disturb his sleeping assistant, who had a smile on his lips. He appeared to be having a sweet dream.

Cooker was enjoying the pleasure of driving and the anticipation of seeing Elisabeth and returning to his offices. Yet as the day went on, his anxiety began to rise. His retreat in a setting as refined at La Tortinière was meant to provide him with needed rest, but he was not feeling rested at all. He thought he could heal himself, but had he chosen the right remedy? The time spent in pampered elegance had only put off the fear of once again being in crowds and dealing with the everyday realities of life. Quick, nervous questions shot through his mind. They were choppy, like the white lines on the highway.

Cooker grew tired of the radio commentator's conventional analysis of the Israel-Palestine situation. He preferred listening to a CD of Marianne Faithfull that was in his glove compartment. The first track was his favorite. It was called "Sleep."

Virgile had curled up on his seat. He grumbled, sounding just like Bacchus, and crossed his arms. Cooker turned up the heat. He, too, was getting cold. Marianne Faithfull's throaty voice reassured him. It was warm and vibrant, melding smoothly into the orchestration.

Virgile mumbled, "Where are we?" He fell back asleep before Cooker had time to answer.

Large clouds rolled over the Charentes region, and a hard rain began to fall. The windshield wipers had trouble keeping up. A sign announced "Next Exit, Saint-Jean-d'Angély." They would be back in Bordeaux in two hours.

When the Mercedes began to shake, Virgile rubbed his eyes, looked at his watch, and then glanced at his boss, who was clearly alarmed. The vibrating was becoming even more pronounced.

"Shit!" Cooker shouted. "What did those bastards do to my car? Was it shaking like this when you drove from Leipzig?"

"No, it was fine, boss," Virgile responded. "Maybe we blew a tire. We should check."

Cooker pulled the car to the side of the road and got out to inspect the tires. All four seemed to be okay.

"We'd better find a service station," Virgile said.

Cooker glanced around and said, "Let's get off at the Saint-Savinien exit. It shouldn't be far now, and I've heard it's got just about the only roadside restaurant worth consideration on this road to Bordeaux. At least we could make the best of a bad situation."

The shaking didn't let up, and the two men stayed alert while Marianne Faithfull kept vigil. To be safe, when they reached the exit, Cooker took the first road after the tollbooth.

They found a service station that no longer sold gas but did do repairs. A rusty sign read "Dollo et Fils." A man in dirty overalls pulled himself out from under a rusty van. He was ageless, wore a felt beret too small for his head and had an engaging smile.

"What can I do for you?"

"Everything!" Cook said, sounding like he believed in miracles.

"What a week. All of Europe seems to be stopping by, and like they say on TV, most of it is breaking down. Yesterday, I saw an old Italian clunker from Fiat. Earlier an English car drove by, right before that a Porsche came in and now more German wheels."

An apprentice with a shaved head was fixing a tire in the corner. There were huge holes in his gauged earlobes. Cooker had seen these outlandishly stretched piercings on other teenagers in Bordeaux. The boss probably didn't like it, Cooker thought, but cheap labor was cheap labor. In this corner of Saintonge, they were not even making good cognac anymore, and customers had to be rare. The winemaker tried to explain the car's symptoms, imitating the wobbling car.

"Is that so?" the mechanic said, brushing his beret to the back of his head. "I bet it's the alignment. Hit a hole in the road maybe?"

Cooker looked accusingly at his assistant. "Did you run into any potholes on your way from Leipzig?"

Virgile shrugged. "I don't think so, boss."

"No worry," the mechanic said. "It's easy to fix. But you're in no hurry, I hope. With a car like that, you must have all the time in the world."

"That is not really the case," Cooker retorted, looking at Virgile. The assistant stood by in silence as the winemaker undertook negotiations that required some diplomacy.

"I don't mean to pry, but what exactly do you do?" the mechanic asked.

Cooker realized that things were turning sour, and he would not be seeing Bordeaux's Tour Pey-Berland so soon.

"I'm a winemaker," Cooker said.

"Are you making those garage wines everyone is talking about these days? You have to tell me how you do it. Maybe it's the wave of the future for *garagistes* like me," the mechanic said with a wink.

Mr. Dollo's face was purple. He clearly liked the fruit of the vine.

"Come on, tell me how you do it, and maybe I'll become a Saint-Émillionnaire and drive a Mercedes myself."

Cooker and Virgile both laughed, and the winemaker saw an opportunity to advance his cause. If he wanted this bizarre individual to focus on his car, he would have to uncork one of the bottles of Vouvray he had picked up in the Loire Valley. The trunk was full of them, and the winemaker liked the idea of using it to grease the mechanic's palm.

"But, sir, before I get to the Mercedes, I gotta finish off the Porsche. The guy's in a hurry and was here before you. It shouldn't take long. Just the belt and the hose. He gave me a nice tip to have it ready this afternoon at four. Know what I mean?" the mechanic said with another wink.

"I believe I do," Cooker said, taking a Taille aux Loups 1993 Clos de Venise from his trunk.

The mechanic grinned and wiped his hands on his overalls.

"I won't say no to that. You're not the kind to run out of gas, that's for sure."

7

At the back of the garage, behind dirty windows and walls decorated with old calendar pinups, sacrilege was occurring. The precious Clos de Venise was foundering in red plastic cups. Virgile had trouble making out the aromas of mangos and pineapple that had enchanted Cooker during the blind tasting some time ago in Amboise.

As rough as he seemed, the mechanic was jovial and even likable. He had improvised a cocktail hour in his office, where oil cans and old tires mixed with a jumble of papers. He thought it polite to serve up stale peanuts in a promotional ashtray.

The mechanic emptied his plastic cup three times, wrinkling his nose and clicking his palate to mimic an expert right under Cooker's nose. The winemaker found it amusing but did not react, hoping that his knowledge of mechanics would surpass his talent as a wine taster.

The mechanic raised his voice and waved a dark, greasy hand to invite his apprentice to join them for the shipwrecked dry Vouvray.

"Come on, taste a little. It'll make a man of you."

The teenager came over and waited for the mechanic to fill his cup. Virgile tried to make conversation, in vain. The boy lifted his cup and emptied it. In one gulp, the clear Vouvray from Montlouis-sur-Loire disappeared. The apprentice held back a burp as he put his cup down. Cooker asked him how old he was, and the mechanic was quick to answer for him. "Sixteen and nothing in the noggin. Just gigantic holes in the ears for the birds to fly through."

The apprentice lowered his head. He managed a small smile as if to apologize for not belonging to the world of adults, and then he made his way behind a wall that served as a closet.

Now that the bottle was empty, and introductions were over, would the mechanic finally decide to get his calloused hands on the convertible? This side trip was taking an unexpected turn. The Cooker-Lanssien team was no longer in a hurry.

The mechanic promised to look at the sick car at the beginning of the afternoon but would not get down to surgery until later in the day, as the Porsche had to get done first.

"He had no wine for me, but he's not too tight-fisted, if you get my drift."

"Oh, yes, I do," Cooker said, adding, "Tell me, my friend, isn't there a place to eat around here of some repute? I can't remember the name."

"Here, all you've got is the truck stop, the Platanes. It's just over there at the intersection," the mechanic said, pointing in the direction of the restaurant. "It's run by Yvette. Nothing fancy, but the steak *à la bordelaise* is good."

"That's the place, Virgile. I recall now, there's not much choice, but they apparently make a mean red wine sauce with just the right amount of bone marrow, butter, and shallots."

The apprentice, who had come out from behind the wall, opened the enormous garage door, which made a loud and annoying squeal as it went up. He had taken off his overalls and was wearing a sweatshirt with English writing on the back. It read "Fuck the boss."

Cooker called out to him, as if he wanted directions, "Hey, kid, what's your name?"

"Rodolphe, sir."

"Nice name," the winemaker said, accompanying the compliment with an unexpected and substantial tip, in another attempt to get the repairs done before day's end.

"Thanks, sir. Have a good meal. You'll see. Yvette is really cool."

As they made their way to the restaurant, Virgile walked with a light step and lifted his nose to sniff the heady odor of wet earth. Cooker stomped along, his head down and his hands deep in his pockets.

Cooker didn't look up until they reached the restaurant parking lot. And parked right in front of him was the beauty with shiny chrome.

"That's Morton's car," Cooker said to Virgile. "I'd recognize it anywhere."

"What did I tell you, boss," Virgile responded. "I said we'd probably meet up with him. But here, in this little hole in the wall, now that's a surprise. And days after he was supposed to be in Bordeaux? I mean, seriously, how does that happen? We break down, take the car to a garage that doesn't sell gas, waste a bottle of Clos de Venise, and find the Morgan at a truck stop."

"Coincidence, my dear Virgile, coincidence. And besides, there really isn't any other place to stop for a decent meal on this road between Tours and Bordeaux. Is it that surprising?"

"What will you say to him? Do you think he knows his girlfriend Oksana is dead?"

"I don't know, Virgile. Why don't we go inside and find him first."

Walking into the restaurant, Cooker scanned the bar and then the dining room, where a waitress was flitting from table to table. Robert Morton was not there.

"Two?"

"Yes, please, miss."

"Near the fireplace?"

"No, next to the man over there."

"As you wish, but you'll be near the door. There are drafts."

"That's fine."

The waitress smiled at Virgile as she handed him the menu.

"A drink, perhaps?"

Having failed to spot Morton, Cooker was in a foul mood. "Two steaks, *à la bordelaise*. How's that, Virgile?"

It was not a good time to contradict his boss, so the assistant responded, "Yes, perfect." Then Virgile tried to smooth things over. "Perhaps he's in the restroom. He'll be out in a minute."

Cooker grumbled.

"Some wine?" the waitress asked. "I could recommend something from the Loire Valley."

"God forbid, no Loire wine," Cooker mumbled under his breath.

"A Château de La Salle, then?"

Virgile nodded at Yvette, who smiled at him in return.

Cooker paid no mind and just complained about the water, which wasn't cold enough. He took a pen out of his pocket and started scribbling on the paper tablecloth. His assistant sat in silence. Cooker imagined that he was just trying to get along.

All things considered, Rodolphe had been right. Yvette was cool. She had long legs, accentuated by shiny heels. Her hips were full, and her heavy breasts swung freely under her shirt.

From where they were sitting, they could hear shouting in the kitchen and smell the hot oil. Cooker examined the other diners, as he kept an eye on the restroom door. He tried to intercept bits of conversation and decrypt their ways of eating, drinking, and speaking. He made a face. Nobody here matched the man who had so appealed to him on the banks of the Indre. Especially the person with the large mole on his left temple who was sitting next to them. The gangly fellow was reading *Le Figaro* and drinking a glass of rosé from Provence. He was wearing tortoiseshell glasses, had a signet ring on his left hand, and he was decked out in a sweater with a horrible multicolored geometric pattern.

Virgile kept following the waitress with his eyes. Cooker couldn't help thinking that the place had gotten its reputation as much from her shape as the steaks.

Their steaks *à la bordelaise* arrived, and Morton was still nowhere to be seen.

"Tell me, Virgile, what do you think of that man drinking rosé next to the wall? No, not that one, to the left."

Virgile remained silent for a while and then said, "Married, around fifty, four children, Catholic, a little noble blood in his veins. He sells corks made in Portugal, has never cheated on his wife, bought a lot of Eurotunnel shares, and is still trying to convince his wife that he's going to earn his investment back. She doesn't really care, because she is sleeping with one of their oldest son's friends. Yes, yes. Gontran's best friend, who teaches her to play golf every Saturday afternoon. She just finished rereading *Ripening Seed* by Colette and says that her husband is a loser and a bad lay, that she has the right to some pleasure, that tomorrow she will definitely leave him, and that her mind is made up. He's entirely preoccupied with the stock market, which is slow to rise, the promise of a vacation with the Arteuil family in their dusty old château in the Poitou, and Eléonore, who is doing her first communion next Sunday. He's a nobody. He can't lie. He doesn't even like nice cars. I bet he drives a Japanese rig that he's still paying off."

Cooker broke out laughing and nearly choked on his Château de La Salle. Some of the other diners, hacking away at their solitude as they emptied their plates, looked at him with disapproval. Cooker felt like he had just become the center of a number of conversations in this lapse from his usual reserve.

Their neighbor on the right got up to leave. Like a fussy old bachelor, he brushed the bread crumbs off his sweater. Cooker noticed his slender fingers and long nails. The man buttoned up his cardigan, adjusted the silk scarf stuffed into the collar of his pale pink shirt, and left a ten-euro tip on a cracked dish. He then carefully folded the receipt and slipped it into his wallet.

Cooker watched him walk out the door and across the parking lot. Then, to Cooker's amazement, the man in the colorful geometric sweater got into the Morgan and started pulling out of the parking lot.

"Quick, Virgile," Cooker yelled, pushing himself away from the table and racing toward the door. By the time they reached the parking lot, the Morgan was speeding down the road.

"That man just took off in Morton's car," Cooker said, out of breath.

"What could have happened, boss? Do you think he stole the car, maybe even before Morton got to Bordeaux? And if he did, what happened to Morton?"

"We're not going to get the answers to those questions now," Cooker said and sighed.

Cooker and Virgile went back into the restaurant, a little embarrassed by the scene they had made when they ran out without paying their check. They returned to their table, figuring they had time to kill before retrieving their car at the Dollo garage. Cooker ordered a cognac and offered his assistant a cigar. Virgile accepted, for once.

"This one should be gentle enough for your delicate palate," Cooker said, carefully cutting off the top of a light-colored and slightly veined wrapper and lighting Virgile's cigar.

"Did you say it was a Santa Damiana?"

Virgile seemed slightly drunk on the cut-hay and dried-alfalfa aromas of the cigar. Just as they did with wine, the smells of his childhood came to the surface.

"Undergrowth, humus, ferns."

Cooker nodded, as he did when he pulled the first olfactory sensations from a glass of wine. Virgile was no longer his assistant, but an applied and determined student.

Virgile continued, hitting his stride. "Pepper, leather, horse manure."

"So far, I agree," Cooker said, puffing his Lusitania. "I think you may be ready for one from Cuba."

"Should I take that as a compliment?"

"Let's just say that you've lost your innocence. Yes, that's it."

A young man in a white toque and stained apron came out of the kitchen and put his arm around the waitress's waist. Yvette adjusted her shirt and simpered at Virgile. Her lipstick had lost some of its shine, and her tight black skirt was hiked up a bit.

The restaurant was now nearly empty, abandoned to the swirls of gray smoke that seemed to stick to the still blades of an old fan. Two cigar butts sat on a blanket of ashes in a shell-shaped ashtray. At this time of day, Cooker and Virgile were no longer wanted here. The cook had removed his toque and had cleared his throat a number of times before saying, "We're closing."

Yvette puckered her lips. "It's not that we're chasing you away or anything, but—"

"It's fine," Cooker said with an amused smile. "It's time for a nap."

Outside, the rain was working the fields again. Cooker walked quickly in an effort to stay dry, and Virgile kept pace. When they arrived at the garage, the Mercedes was right where they had left it. Cooker felt his temple begin to throb as he faced the prospect of spending even more time waiting for his car. The mechanic came out of his office. He wiped his forehead with the back of his sleeve.

"Don't get worked up, now," he said. "The Porsche is done, and I can get going on the Mercedes. Out of alignment. I knew it. Must have been a hole in the road, like I said, eh?"

He went back into his office and came out again, carrying a grimy dog-eared book with "Mercedes" written on the cover.

"You're in luck, my friends. I still have the manual for your vintage car."

He opened it, and Cooker watched as he checked the calibrations for the wheels.

"Two hours, and you're on the way back home. One hour, if you must hurry. The Porsche owner, he was in the hurry, and he was not cheap."

8

In Bordeaux, the Place Saint-Michel was the site of an odd makeshift setup that morning. Antique vendors fought gusts of wind to raise their gigantic green-and-yellow parasols. Large drops of rain coming from the west jeopardized an improvised Oriental carpet sale. Cautious vendors covered their goods with see-through tarps. There were few passersby, and little chance of making a deal.

Cooker made his way quickly through the flea market without even glancing at the stands. He nodded at a few vendors with whom he sometimes haggled for still lifes, winemaking tools, old postcards, and mismatched crystal glasses.

His coat collar was up around his ears, and he took care not to slip on the cobblestone walkways in the Saint Pierre neighborhood. He turned on the Rue Saint-Rémi, stopping at the Grand Théâtre newsstand, where he intended to get back into his old routine.

"Hello Mrs. Camensac," he said. "I'd like the *Sud-Ouest*, *Le Figaro*, the *RVF*, and the *Herald*

Tribune, please. Nasty weather, isn't it?" And then he headed up the Allées de Tourny.

He paused when he reached number 46. The copper plaque that read "Cooker & Co." was dripping in the rain. The bronze doorbell was still shiny, but he would have to paint the door next spring. He pushed open the porte-cochère.

Nothing had changed. Benjamin Cooker had not been in his offices for over a month. The staircase felt steeper, and he had to stop on the landing to catch his breath. He would not admit it, but he was nervous about getting back to work. It took his secretary Jacqueline's candid smile, purple suit, and perfect education to dissipate his anxiety. How could he have forgotten the heady smell of beeswax that always hovered in his somewhat quaint offices? And the discreet whistle of the kettle that Miss Delmas used for her god-awful herbal teas? If only he could convert her to regular tea.

"Mr. Lanssien will swing by around ten this morning," Jacqueline said, helping her boss with his rain-logged Loden.

"Mr. Cooker, I arranged all your mail in file folders on your desk," she said, spreading his jacket over two coat hooks.

"Thank you, Jacqueline. What would I do without you?"

Several piles of letters awaited him on the Empire-style desk. A carefully tied package was sitting next to his old Napoleon III inkstand. A felt-tip marker had been used to write "Personal" on the outside. The handwriting was thick and contorted. Cooker looked for the sender's address but found nothing. He ripped off the brown paper wrapping. Inside, he found his notebook.

He examined the packaging again and found a postmark. It was the only clue: the notebook had been sent three days earlier from the Champigny-sur-Marne post office. In the end, it did not really matter, now that he had recovered his car and his precious notebook. He called Elisabeth right away. She suggested that they celebrate the event at noon at the restaurant Noailles.

"That is, unless you invite me to the Saint James in Bouliac."

"Done deal," Cooker said, rubbing his cigar box before pulling out a D Number 4 from Partagas.

The wall clock hanging above the mantel had just announced ten o'clock when Virgile barged into Cooker's office. His coat was too big for him, and he looked pale. He wore a colorful turtle-neck, and dark bags under his eyes indicated that his night had been too short. He plopped into an armchair in front of the desk and registered his boss's good humor.

With gray cigar smoke encircling his head, Cooker was busy putting checkmarks on some of the letters encumbering his desk. He removed his reading glasses, which gave him a certain professorial look, and told Virgile about the fine surprise that had been waiting for him. The winemaker had to cut his story short, though, when an unexpected visitor stuck his head in the door.

"Hubert! What brings you to Bordeaux?"

The owner of the Château Angélus did not look his best.

"Come in. You know Virgile, my assistant, don't you?"

Hubert de Boüard shook the young man's hand. His friendship with Cooker was longstanding, and there had never been any snags. Angélus got fantastic notations in the *Cooker Guide*, especially after the premier grand cru heir took on the services of the renowned winemaker Michel Rolland while also following the less official advice of his friend Cooker. The two men had a very cordial friendship and shared a passion for Cuban cigars.

"What are you smoking at this hour of the day, old devil?" Hubert asked.

"A D4, as you can see. It's a bit strong, but the day has gotten off to a good start. My tasting notes that were stolen in Paris came back to me in the mail. I don't know if it was the thief or a Good Samaritan who found it somewhere. I suspect it's the latter. It's comforting to know that someone, somewhere took the time to wrap it, stick postage on it, and drop it in a mailbox. And to do so without asking for a dime, but just because it was the right thing to do. You see, Hubert, acts like that make me believe in people."

"I'm really very happy for you, Benjamin."

"I can assure you right away. Angélus got a good rating in the new guide," the winemaker said. "You, of course, know how highly I regard your 2000 vintage. Perhaps you would like to know the final score I gave it, unless you've come to tell me you got another mysterious message."

"That's exactly it," Hubert de Boüard said, holding the white envelope out to his friend.

Virgile leaned in as Cooker examined the address. Biting his lip, he said, "This friend of yours might be a neighbor. The card was sent from Saint-Émilion yesterday."

"That is what worries me," Hubert said.

The tick-tock of the clock was the only sound in the room. With just enough affectation, Cooker set his cigar down in a white porcelain ashtray. He removed the card from the envelope and read the terse message: "Cave de l'Angélus. Does that ring a bell?" Then, in all capital letters, "AND THREE FOR ME."

Cooker quickly closed the card, as it was clearly disturbing his friend, one of Saint-Émilion's most emblematic winemakers.

"Now, Hubert, I'm afraid you have no choice. You have to tell the cops. When did you get it?"

"In the morning mail."

"Virgile, were there any break-ins on the news last night or today?"

"Not that I know of, sir."

"Did you listen to the radio this morning?"

"Yes, well, no, I mean, not exactly."

"So actually, you aren't really awake. Go home and take a good shower, and this afternoon I want a detailed list of all the wine auctions planned for the next month."

"Throughout France?"

"France and beyond, including London, New York, and Geneva. Is that clear?"

"Yes, sir."

"Oh, and I almost forgot. Tell your lady of the moment to give you a break. Don't forget to mention that your boss is back from vacation."

Cooker's sudden frivolity seemed to cheer Hubert de Boüard up a bit. He put his cigar back in his mouth and took two puffs before reading the morning newspapers with his friend. The Angélus gang had not struck again. Or at least not yet.

§ § §

An hour later, Elisabeth Cooker walked into her husband's office without knocking. Cooker knew that she rarely did this, and it reflected just how happy she was that he had recovered his notebook. She greeted the Angélus estate owner with effusive kisses on his cheeks.

"What? Where's the champagne?"

"True, after all, why not?" Cooker said affably.

"Jacqueline, please, four champagne glasses. Let's uncork that Dom Pérignon that's been waiting in the storeroom refrigerator."

They all raised a toast to Cooker's health, the returned notebook, the rating given to the 2000 Angélus, and all others who praised that exceptional wine. Hubert forgot his worries and promised to drop the three cards off at the Libourne police station. Cooker invited him to join them at the Saint James for lunch.

"Hubert, I'm sure it's just some bad joke. You need to get your mind off it. A good meal is exactly what you need."

"I don't want to get in the way of you two lovebirds."

"Oh come on, you're like family."

The three friends crossed the Allées de Tourny under a golf umbrella to reach Hubert de Boüard's Range Rover, which was double parked on the Rue de Sèze. A soppy, barely legible parking ticket on the windshield did not even dampen the trio's mood.

"Some more mail," Cooker said with a smirk.

§ § §

Lunch at the Saint James lasted well into the afternoon. It was a pretext for the head sommelier to get the famous and expert diners to taste some of his wines. Elisabeth listened, tasted, and added her two cents. She seemed happy to see that her husband's enthusiasm had returned. In the restaurant parking lot, Cooker contemplated not returning to his office and going home to enjoy Grangebelle under the rain. He pictured a fire in the fireplace, Bacchus at his feet, a call to Margaux—it was only noon in New York—and a cup of Nepalese tea, the one his tea-loving friend Gilles Brochard had sent him.

Then he changed his mind. He had too much work to do. Hundreds of tasting samples awaited him, and he needed to swing by the lab and make sure Alexandrine de la Palussière was on those cases of eutypiosis in the Côtes du Marmandais and the Entre-Deux-Mers. The vines were rotting, and radical treatment was needed. New regulations forbade the use of sodium arsenite. Virgile would have to monitor the endemic proliferation of the damned fungus that was eating away at the vine stock. No French vineyard had been spared. And the recent rain was not helping. It was pruning season, and shears propagated the

infection. Naturally, Cooker & Co. recommended the intensive use of a fungicide like benomyl
to at least contain the spread, but that required
time and a lot of meticulous work. His office
was drowning in calls for help, and dawdling at
home would be criminal. Cooker was starting to
feel guilty.

He gave Elisabeth a tender kiss and reassured
her that he would be all right. On the left bank
of the Garonne River, behind a curtain of rain,
Bordeaux looked like a bad watercolor. Cooker
would have to face the traffic on the Pont de Pierre.
When would the work be done on the tramway?

§ § §

Cooker did not recognize him at first. Wearing
an off-white raincoat, a long woolen scarf, and
a checked hunting cap, the man looked like a
wading bird emerging from a marsh. He was
waiting in the reception area. When he saw the
winemaker, he smiled to hide his discomfort.

"This gentleman has been here since the beginning of the afternoon," Jacqueline was quick
to say. "He would like to see you. He says he
knows you."

"We do know each other, in fact," Cooker said. "Please come in, Mr. Morton."

The visitor had clearly left behind the self-assurance and elegance that had so appealed to Cooker at La Tortinière. He seemed hesitant. He talked in starts, and his outfit was ordinary, to say the least.

"Please, do sit down," the winemaker said, with a touch of condescension. The man looked clearly bothered by something.

Cooker examined him, his gaze lingering conspicuously on Morton's shoes, which were very well-polished loafers with worn-down heels. He guessed the size to be forty-three, perhaps forty-four.

"Would you like a whisky, my dear man?"

"No, thank you," said the intruder, who did not remove his raincoat.

"It's been awhile since our stay at La Tortinière. I'd say a lot has happened since, hasn't it?"

Morton sank into the armchair. He was very pale, and his features were tense.

"What about a Macallan 1946 from my personal collection?"

"That would be hard to refuse," Morton said.

Cooker filled two finely chiseled glasses.

"Thank you, Benjamin. Do you mind if I still call you Benjamin?"

"Why would I mind?"

"Because you must think that you have a murderer sitting in front of you."

"Why would I be thinking that?" Cooker asked, barely sipping his whisky. "As far as I'm aware, you drove off in your Morgan long before Oksana's body was found. And, by the way, I spotted your Morgan in a small town about two hours from Bordeaux. Someone else was driving it. Was it stolen?"

Cooker noted the surprised look on Morton's face. He seemed to be fumbling for an answer.

"Why, uh, yes," he said. "It was stolen. I've reported it to the police. You spotted it? I'll have to tell them. But I'm not here about the car. I'm here to convince you that I had nothing to do with Oksana's death."

"I'm listening."

The Englishman took a swig of the Scottish malt, and it seemed to revive him. He unbuttoned his raincoat and untied his scarf.

"I didn't kill Oksana or the concierge—and yes, I do know that he was found hanging from a tree. Please, Benjamin, don't doubt what I'm saying."

"I would like nothing more than to believe you, Robert. But your name is not Robert, is it? Nor is it Morton?"

"How do you know?"

"I'm not one to confuse a Bordeaux wine with a Burgundy. The same goes for my friends. I'm quick to separate the wheat from the chaff."

"Where do you put me?"

"For now, among people who need help. That is, if you give me some proof of your good faith, starting with your real identity."

"My name is James Welling and—"

"You were not born in London, were you?"

"That's right. I come from Canterbury."

"That might explain your ease at telling tales."

The Englishman smiled. He had never read Chaucer, confessed his ignorance, and promised to remedy it someday.

"I won't ask that much of you," Cooker grumbled. "Did you know that Geoffrey Chaucer was the son of one of London's largest wine merchants?"

"No, I didn't."

"Are you at least a wine broker?"

"Well, yes and no."

"If you want to stay friends with me, you had better start giving some straight answers."

"Let's just say that I work in wine, but more with collectors and enlightened connoisseurs."

"I had noted that vinegar is not your cup of tea and that you don't wipe your mouth with your sleeve when you eat."

"I get it from my father. When I was a teenager, he let me taste great wines like Château Haut-Brion, Romanée-Conti, Pétrus, Cheval Blanc, and even Ruster Ausbruch."

A man who knew that intriguingly sweet, refreshing, and elegant Austrian wine could not be all bad. Morton—or rather Welling—was starting to look just a bit better. Cooker put his glass of fifty-year-old Macallan to his nose and listened to the man, who was going on about the wines he had sampled during his formative years.

The list was long. For each estate, Welling supplied the vintage without any hesitation. He had an infallible memory. "1961 Margaux, 1967 Yquem, 1955 Mission Haut-Brion, 1959 Lafite-Rothschild, 1982 Pétrus, 1983 Montrachet."

Cooker's eyes glistened as Welling enumerated the mythic vintages. He was having a hard time concealing his jealousy. They ended up finding a shared memory, a 1961 Hermitage La Chapelle.

"It was as dark as ink, but what fruit!" Welling said.

"I remember aromas of cooked prunes," Cooker said, excited to be recalling these sensations.

Welling became more animated, and his sentences were sharper. A rebellious lock of hair on his forehead made him look mischievous and even a little precious. His signet ring shone in the glow of Cooker's desk lamp. Dusk was spreading across the city.

"You deliberately left the Loire wines off your inventory. That would certainly bring us back to the reason for today's visit, would it not? Didn't we say we'd share a Bonnezeaux when we were at Château d'Artigny?" Cooker asked, winking to look sly.

"I always honor my promises, Benjamin."

And like a magician, Welling slid his hand into the inside pocket of his gabardine and pulled out a bottle of the golden liquid.

"Les Deux Allées, Château de Fesles, 1995. How's that for you, grand master?"

"A lesser bottle would have done the trick. I like that you keep your word. That's a sign of integrity. Speaking of which, I'm curious about what you did when you left La Tortinière after learning that your companion, or should I say, your plaything, had taken off."

The Englishman looked down, cleared his throat twice, swallowed a mouthful of Macallan, and held his glass in the palms of his hands, as if he were trying to warm it.

"That is exactly why I am here."

Welling stood and started pacing without looking at Cooker. He told his story from start to finish without omitting any details, which seemed to give some credence to what could have appeared unseemly.

Yes, that night, he was supposed to go to Bordeaux. The girl had been a prostitute, but she had wounded his ego by leaving him, and he didn't feel like driving all the way to Bordeaux right away. So he drove his Morgan to Tours. He parked not far from the police station and took a long walk along the Quai d'Orléans. He ended up in the Jardin François Premier. From there, he went into a sordid cabaret, where strippers were putting on such a pathetic show, he had no choice but to down five or maybe six brandies. That was when one of the other customers came up to the bar and started looking for trouble. They called him damned Rosbeef and son of a bitch. They slapped him around. Afterward? He did not really remember. He woke up groggy in front of some townhouse, with blood on his face and a sore back.

Cooker felt like lighting a cigar but decided to play with his pen instead. He did a sketch of Welling in blue ink. Sketching was a skill that dated back three decades to the one year he had spent at art school in Paris. When his visitor fell silent, he encouraged him.

"And then?"

"Then I wanted to go back to my car, but I couldn't remember where I had parked it. So I paced up and down the street along the river until I was exhausted. I was devastated. That's when I saw them locked in an embrace on the embankment. He was kissing her neck, and she was responding. I just stood there. I didn't curse or threaten. I tried to yell, but nothing came out. I was speechless. I was trembling. I was freezing to death."

The winemaker was concentrating on getting Welling's slightly protruding chin just right, when he noticed that the man was shaking. His monologue was not as smooth anymore.

"Then, after giving me one of her looks—you remember Oksana's looks, right?—she said to the guy, 'Let's get out of here. There's another drunk.' I can still hear them laughing as they made their way down the steps toward the river. They started to run and disappeared under the bridge."

Welling was now looking out the window. Cooker knew his back was turned because he was hiding his tears.

"Was it the boy Gaétan, the hotel concierge?"

"I couldn't tell, really. I barely saw them."

"What about his size and his hair?" Cooker pressed, growing just a little annoyed by the show of emotion.

"Yes, I think it was him."

"And then?"

"And then? Two men approached me. One was small, and the other one was brawny, I would say. They asked me if I knew the girl. They had a thick Central European accent."

"What did you tell them?" Cooker asked.

"I shook my head."

"Why?"

"I don't know. Maybe I was afraid for her. Or for me."

"They took off down the stairs and disappeared under the bridge."

"What did you do then?"

"Nothing."

"Did you hear screams?"

"Nothing, Benjamin, I swear."

"I'm not the one you should be swearing to. It should be the police. And quickly. You know you're a major suspect, right?"

Welling finally turned around. He wiped his tears on his sleeve and mumbled, "First, I had to confide in you. You are the only friend I have in this country."

The winemaker did not like being a confidant in this way. He set aside the pad where he had drawn the very touching Welling, who did not look at all like that dashing Morton from La Tortinière. He then poured some more whisky in Welling's glass.

"1946. Can you imagine, Benjamin, that's the year I was born."

"Should I believe you?"

Welling showed him an old, dog-eared passport with a picture of a man wearing glasses. Next to it was his very British pedigree: James Cornelius John Welling. Date of birth: 15 August 1946. Place of birth: Canterbury, Kent.

Now that the Englishman had revealed his real name and shared his memory of all those fine wines, Cooker liked him again.

"So, should we open that Fesles?" Welling asked, as if to test Cooker's trust.

"No, tomorrow evening, at the same time, once you've told the police everything."

9

Virgile resigned himself to completing the task assigned to him. The job was painstaking, enormous, and thankless, but he could not disobey Benjamin Cooker. With the boss back, excitement was returning to the lab on the Cours du Chapeau-Rouge and the offices on the Allées de Tourny. Virgile retired to a small room to make a systematic list of wine auctions, beginning with those in Bordeaux's Chartrons neighborhood. He called the heads of Dubourg, Cazaux, Dubern, Bricadieu, Courau, and Le Blay. They were all overly courteous and gave him a list of the stocks they would be auctioning. He did the same with Mr. Poulin and Mr. Le Fur in Paris. He also consulted Tajan et Artus Associés, along with Catherine Charbonneaux, who was one of Cooker's friends. In his zeal, he made the rounds of France's other wine auctions, estate by estate, château by château. He did not think he would get through it in a day. The man who assigned him the tireless task did, however, refrain from harassing his "secretary." Gratitude was not the least of Cooker's qualities.

The next day, Virgile set a thick stack of papers on Cooker's desk, like a bearer of bad news expecting to be shot.

"No stocks of Angélus anywhere?" Cooker asked.

"Just six bottles by Mr. Galateau in Limoges, twelve at Sabourin in Châtellerault, and two cases of six with Besh in Cannes. Nothing to get excited about," Virgile responded, reading disappointment on the winemaker's face.

But Cooker paused as he went over the list. He put on his reading glasses and underlined one item twice. Then, after a long sigh, he smiled at his assistant and said, "Tell Jacqueline to call in an offer on the 1961 Pape Clément for, say, a hundred euros a bottle. Add the case of six 1985 Mazis-Chambertin for, well, two hundred euros, give or take fifty. Okay?"

"You got it, boss."

"At least your work wasn't a total waste of time."

Virgile scowled, took his papers, and started walking away. He was not wearing the kind and attractive expression that had worked so well on Elisabeth Cooker the day he had arrived at Grangebelle for his job interview.

"What's bothering you, Virgile? A heartbreak?"

"Just a break, that's all."

The winemaker did not want to pry. He knew he could put his foot in his mouth. He decided to stand up and survey the activity on the Allées de Tourny, where carnival workers were taking down a merry-go-round. Having second thoughts, he moved closer to his assistant.

"Nothing serious, I hope."

"It's my little sister, Raphaëlle. She—"

Virgile stared at the empty carousel that no longer had its wooden horses. His eyes filled with tears. Cooker put a hand on the young man's shoulder.

"What is it?"

"She's got cancer. Colon cancer. It doesn't look good."

Virgile started sobbing. "Tell me she's not going to die."

"Virgile, I can't tell you what you want to hear. I will pray for her."

"Like that will help."

"Would you rather resign yourself to her dying?"

"That's not what I mean, Mr. Cooker."

The two men looked at each other. The telephone rang twice, and Cooker ignored it. His secretary knocked on the door.

"Just a minute Jacqueline, please."

At that moment, nothing was more pressing than the needs of his distressed assistant. This worthy son of a winemaker with such an earnest look seemed ready to collapse. Cooker knew that at twenty-five, death was not a looming prospect, but instead a far-off eventuality.

"Come on, Virgile. I think we have better things to do than pour out our feelings to each other. I don't think Raphaëlle would like that. Actually, I'm sure she wouldn't."

After a long silence and a gesture of tenderness that could have been that of a father to a son, the winemaker added, "I have hope for her."

Virgile dried his cheeks, the way he must have on winter mornings when he walked to school in Montravel, and the cold wind stung his eyes until he cried. He looked like a little boy again. The same little boy who used his sleeve to wipe blood from his nose when he fought like a devil in the schoolyard with a bully who cheated at marbles. Virgile always said that in the Lanssien family, there was "no sniveling, even when you bury your mom and pop." How many times had his father called him a pussy when he crawled into his mother's arms to cry? Would he cry on his father's grave one day? This was the same father who had not seen Raphaëlle since she had taken up with a divorced man who was fifteen years older than she.

§ § §

When Cooker and his assistant left 46 Allées de Tourny, the merry-go-round had been completely dismantled. Shy rays of sunlight were trying to revive a city mired in winter. One could barely make out Lormont through the thick fog that refused to lift off the Garonne, rusting its pontoons and barges. The two men slipped into the convertible that was parked on the quays. The tramway had opened up recently in this part of town and now reigned over public transportation in Bordeaux. Virgile took it frequently, but Cooker refused. "Perhaps one day," he had said without an ounce of conviction.

"Head to Saint-Macaire" was all that Cooker said. For once, he refrained from turning on the radio or playing one of the opera openings that exasperated Virgile.

"Mission?"

"Château Fayard."

"Isn't Jacques-Charles de Musset one of your favorites in the upcoming guide?"

"Exactly. It's a small estate, just over seventeen acres and about a dozen barrels of a dry white every year. Beyond reproach," Cooker said.

"Yes, I tasted a few samples at the lab," Virgile added.

"And?"

"Sweet."

"Virgile, what is this hip language you're using? Sweet. You don't call a dry white wine "sweet."

That's like saying a wine is "good." If it's not good, there's no reason to talk about it, and if it's good you drink it and *describe* it."

Cooker was getting worked up, as only he knew how to do. He could throw a fit at a moment's notice and then get over it just as quickly. Truth be told, Cooker was just trying to divert Virgile from his sad thoughts, and he wondered if his assistant was fooled by the tactic.

"In Fayard, there are vines that are over sixty years old, with yields of—"

"Around five hundred and twenty gallons every two and a half acres. And the vines are fertilized with horse crap."

"How do you know that, Virgile?"

"Four years ago, I harvested there. It was, well, let's just say it was more than good."

"Well then, say it was outstanding." Cooker saw his assistant smile for the first time that day.

Layers of fog covered the river as the elegant Château Fayard rose from the rows of vines that winter had transformed into sad, bony skeletons.

Virgile dug up his memories from the harvest and shared them with Cooker. The laughter among the grapevines, T-shirts splotched with red, hands stiff from intensive use of pruning sheers, and backs stooped from days of going from row to row, heads down and cutters in hand.

Virgile seemed very happy to see Jacques-Charles de Musset again. Of course, he remembered Virgile. He even remembered that the young man had followed around a Swedish girl named Ingrid. She had aquamarine eyes and hair as golden as Semillon grapes. It was one of a thousand flirtations that had no tomorrows. It was just the way of the harvest: hard work, schoolboy pranks, girls in tank tops, boys in their prime, juicy clusters of grapes, sweet lips, and uncalled-for gestures covered up by the laughter of old-timers who made sure nobody dawdled. That was four years ago, the year Raphaëlle fled Montravel to live her life in Périgueux. Virgile loved his sister. And to think that…

"No, that is very kind of you, but we have other plans. Another time, perhaps. Thank you for the case."

Cooker said good-bye to the head of Fayard with a firm, friendly handshake that Virgile clumsily tried to imitate. His heart was not in it. That was too bad, because he had fond memories of the Saint Macaire harvest, mixed with a few regrets. Why had he not bedded that beautiful Ingrid?

As they drove back to Bordeaux, Cooker tried to find out more about the pretty Scandinavian who had captivated his assistant. Virgile refused to answer his questions and remained silent, looking out over the dark waters of the Garonne.

On the way, Cooker made a sharp turn to the right. The tires screeched, and Virgile gave his driver the evil eye. Cooker did not blink as he stepped on the clutch and changed gears. A few minutes later, the Mercedes stopped at the Place du Verdelais. There was not a soul on the walkways, which looked like they belonged in an old spa town where people went to treat melancholy as much as rheumatism. The village looked dead. What inhabitants remained must be working or napping this afternoon. All around the square, abandoned shops had bygone signs. The only hotel had given up. A gigantic basilica seemed to crush the houses that pushed against its base. A golden Mother Mary perched on the steeple overlooked the whole. Cooker thought about Montbazon.

Virgile buried his chin in his jacket. A cold wind whisked brightly colored papers off the ground. They announced a raffle in Saint Maixent: "Win a wide-screen TV, ten fat ducks, two stag legs, and other prizes. Do not litter."

"What are we doing here?" Virgile grumbled.

The winemaker did not respond and walked toward the basilica. Virgile followed in silence.

The smell of melted wax floated in the dark air. The walls were covered with ex-votos dedicated to Our Lady of Verdelais, known for miraculous healing and miraculous good works. Cooker made the sign of the cross and walked down the central aisle, illuminated by a few flickering candles, past a woman who was praying.

As he knelt at the front of the church, Cooker recalled the Angélus devotion. He wondered how many times the homage to the Blessed Mother and the Annunciation had been recited in this ancient place. How many times had the Angélus bell rung at six in the morning, noon and six in the evening? It was a ritual followed in Catholic churches all over the world.

Cooker thought Virgile would be lurking somewhere in the back of the church. And, in fact, his assistant was hovering like a naughty imp near a confessional that had probably not seen a sinner in decades. From this observation point, Virgile watched his boss's somewhat abstruse actions. He seemed impressed with Cooker's devotion, although he himself did not believe in God anymore than he believed in himself. Nobody had taught him how, not even his mother, who had been raised by nuns.

Cooker buried his face in his hands for a long time and then stood up and lit a votive candle. Virgile, still huddled near the old confessional, stared at the flame. He shivered. He must be thinking about Raphaëlle, perhaps saying a clumsy prayer, begging the plaster Lady of Verdelais statue, which was dressed like some Oriental doll as she looked down on him from her pedestal. The church bells broke the frozen silence. Cooker made the sign of the cross again and joined Virgile on the square outside the church. The young man's eyes were red.

"I don't believe in that stuff, sir."

"You're lying. I saw you praying near the confessional."

"I wasn't praying. I was crying."

"It's the same thing," Cooker said. "You cry when you think God has abandoned you. Even Christ experienced doubt on the cross. You have no reason to doubt, or you might as well just change jobs, my dear Virgile."

"Never."

"Show the same faith in the unknown as you have in things related to wine."

This was one of the occasions when student and teacher dared to explore the meandering path of religious belief. They talked for what seemed like hours about philosophy and theology while following the stations of the cross that rose above the Garonne Valley. The two pilgrims braved the west wind and the light rain that seeped into their bones, and for a while, they forgot their ages, their health, their ambitions, and perhaps even their own convictions. Then the Verdelais church bells struck five.

"Oh dear," Cooker said. "I forgot to call Hubert de Boüard. Come on, let's go to Saint-Émilion."

10

Along the ridge, the thick forests of the Landes blocked the horizon. The ashen sky darkened suddenly in a call for night to come. Cooker was happy to let his assistant drive the Mercedes. Their long discussion had exhausted him. He asked Virgile to put on the high beams. "The roads are treacherous here," he said.

Saint-Émilion was only three-quarters of an hour away. As they drove through Saint-Germain-de-Grave, Cooker pointed out the former Sisters of the Assumption convent, which had been converted to a wine estate a century earlier.

"The Château des Mille Anges—château of a thousand angels," Cooker said.

"Did you count them?" Virgile asked.

"A lot of them didn't show up, apparently. But you know as well as I do that angels never miss out on taking their share of drink."

Virgile rolled his eyes at this vintner reference to the portion of wine that evaporates in oak barrels. He stepped on the gas pedal.

"Virgile, we're not in any hurry. Stop here, would you?"

Before the shadows took hold of the hills and valleys that outlined the Bordeaux Premières Côtes, Cooker pointed his elegant index finger at the line of cypress trees that led to Malagar, a home that author François Mauriac had held dear.

"Look, there is the Maromé castle, which Toulouse-Lautrec liked so much," Virgile said, glancing at Cooker with a smirk.

Cooker was blown away. *Who was being the professor now?* His assistant was no angel and took an evil pleasure in rebuffing people who were too full of themselves. Virgile continued: "And there is the Domaine du Cheval Blanc, which shouldn't be confused with the Château Cheval-Blanc, which belongs to your friends Bernard Arnaud and Albert Frère. Isn't that right, master?"

"It won't be so much fun if I have nothing left to teach you."

"But you did teach me a lot today."

Virgile looked up at the sky, which was sadly lacking stars. But lights were shimmering at Génisson, Grand Housteau, Âtre Étoilé, and Grang Garron, estates whose wines Cooker knew well, not only because he had tasted them, but also because he had made some of them. The winemaker had a respectful word for each of these domains shining on the hills. As the night slowly took possession of the acres of vineyards, they shared a moment of wordless private pleasure. Was it still a decent hour to be visiting Angélus?

Cooker's cell phone rang, interrupting the moment of grace and satisfaction the two men were enjoying.

"Cooker here."

"It's Welling. Am I bothering you?"

"Yes, I mean no. What's new?"

"I have to see you. It's urgent."

"Okay. In my office, tomorrow, around, say, eleven."

"What about tonight?"

"Listen, James, I'm in the middle of an assessment."

"Can I come and join you?"

"Well, actually—"

Virgile could see that his employer was becoming entangled in ridiculous lies. Annoyed, Cooker finally said, "Okay, listen, be at the Café Français in an hour. No, I will not be alone. Yes, that's right, my assistant will be with me."

He hung up, angry with his caller. "What a bore."

Virgile waited for his boss to give some explanation. It was long in coming, but then Cooker told the story of Welling's visit to the office, from beginning to end. He recounted every detail. The winemaker had believed what the strange man had said.

"Why, then, did he lie to you at La Tortinière?" Virgile asked.

"For love of wine!"

"That's a little simplistic."

"He's a collector, Virgile. A fabulous collector. He has tasted the best wines the world has to offer. I suspect he is rich and passes much of his time traveling the globe, putting together the best wine collection one could ever imagine."

"Is that an end in itself?"

"You're becoming philosophical, Virgile."

"You're contagious, sir."

Cooker furrowed his brow, which in him was an indication that he was pleased. He liked the compliment.

"What exactly is he doing in Bordeaux?" Virgile asked.

"I admit that I didn't ask him," Cooker confessed, uncomfortable at being found out by his own student.

"It can't be an auction that's on his mind. That's for sure," Virgile said, still a little annoyed by the previous day's assignment.

"We'll know in less than an hour."

"Unless he serves up another one of stories he's so good at when he sits down to eat," Virgile said.

"I promise you, Virgile, you'll want to make his acquaintance."

"If you say so, sir."

§ § §

Cooker wondered why he didn't go to the Café Français more often. This Bordeaux brasserie had the kind of old-world charm that had captivated him when he was an art student in the capital, cultivating refined idleness on the Boulevard Saint-Germain. The copper work was as shiny as it could get. The booths were comfortable, and the staff was friendly without overdoing it.

As an aesthete, Cooker chose the moleskine booth without hesitation. He could see the proud Saint André cathedral from there. Each of its dizzying pinnacles was lit up like a Christmas tree. In the middle of this extravagance of light, the Tour Pey-Berland was not to be outdone. The statue of the Virgin Mary on its steeple had been covered in gold leaf. This stone theater was outrageously flashy. Bordeaux had suffered far too long from the plague that had eaten away at its eighteenth-century façades and had every reason to be happy with its recent face-lift. The city shone anew and was experiencing a renaissance. Cooker was among those who were pleased. The city was like its wines and deserved to have its reputation supported at all cost, even if it meant a little artifice.

Welling did not spoil the scene. He was wearing a duffle coat that, with his graying hair, made him appear somewhat lost in the modern world. He removed it with such a pronounced British flair, the effect was almost theatrical. Welling gave Virgile his best smile and shook Cooker's hand warmly. They each said they were dying of hunger and unrolled their napkins without waiting. Straight out, the Englishman ordered a 1988 Canon la Gaffelière. Then the waiter sent an order for three *entrecôtes*, rare, to the kitchen.

"Perhaps some mineral water?" the waiter asked.

"I think I was clear, young man," Welling answered.

"Could there be a teetotaler among us?" Cooker added.

The waiter put on a poker face and held up his order pad.

"A what?" Virgile asked, hardly fooled by his boss's act.

"A teetotaler," Cooker pontificated. "A race of individuals not to be recommended, incapable of communicating about wine, with a natural repugnance for alcohol."

The three diners broke out laughing. The waiter timidly joined in.

He filled their glasses with Saint-Émilion, which exhaled Oriental spices. Cooker noted aromas of cooked cassis. Virgile added cedar, while

Welling, who chose his words carefully and spoke with affectation, mentioned smoked oak. What followed was a tasting by experts that intrigued the couple sitting to their left. The woman looked like she was soaking up Cooker's words. She and her companion did not appear well-suited for each other, but this evening, they shared curiosity. Restaurants always seemed to be full of bored couples who enjoyed eavesdropping.

"Welling, you are looking well since you gave yourself up to the police."

"Did you know that they weren't even looking for me? I wasn't even a suspect."

"Thanks to your feet," Cooker said.

"What do you mean?" Welling asked, pausing his knife above his steak.

Virgile was wolfing down his shallot-topped meat between mouthfuls of grand cru classé. The winemaker, distilling his deductions like an old rusty alembic, did not say much. His astuteness excited Welling, who emptied his glass of Canon-la-Gaffelière rather quickly. As Cooker explained how he had been exonerated in the Oksana case and then in the disguised suicide of the concierge, Welling tossed in "that's right" after each forkful.

"There's no hiding anything from you, Benjamin. It's as if you were there when I talked to that cops. Do you know the captain?"

125

"A little," the winemaker said evasively, eyeing his seemingly passive assistant. "But tell me, James, you didn't really invite me here to tell me what I already know."

"No, but to let you in on a good deal. It's the least I can do for you. A private sale tomorrow. Nothing but treasures. Marvels, I assure you."

"Like what?" Cooker asked.

"For starters, 1955 and 1975 Pétrus, 1983 Margaux, 1989 and 1995 Latour, 1995 Ducru-Beaucaillou, 1989 Cos d'Estournel, 1998 Calon-Ségur, 1996 Pichon-Longueville, 1970 Conseillante, 1977 Pape Clément, 1990 Talbot, among others."

"Stop, stop, my cellar is already full," Cooker said, trying to conceal the disillusionment in his voice. This list was worthy of a forger. "A private sale, you say?"

"Yes, I'm in cahoots with the Belgian broker I stood up on the night Oksana walked out on me. We have an appointment tomorrow morning at the Hôtel de Villesèque."

Virgile, who had so far been quiet, nervously pulled off his sweater, as though the Canon-la-Gaffelière was making him too hot. He asked the waiter for water.

"Mineral water, please."

Welling and Cooker both stared at him. Virgile responded, "Sirs, I now am joining the teetotalers."

"You know, Virgile, that could get you fired," Cooker said.

"Wait until tomorrow afternoon before doing the paperwork," Virgile said with youthful arrogance. "Mr. Welling, could I tag along tomorrow?"

"Why would you like to do that?" the Englishman asked.

"To see those labels."

"I'm afraid that will not be possible," Welling answered, looking very sorry. "This kind of event requires the greatest confidentiality, and Mr. Wolvertem, my Belgian broker, would certainly not want you there."

"Tell me, James, how did you meet this, well, this broker of the finest and rarest wines?" Cooker asked, articulating each word.

"On the Internet, Benjamin. I may be driving a Morgan, but I am a modern man. I take only the best from the past. That is my philosophy."

"I have no doubt," Cooker said.

"How many customers like you does your Mr. Wolvertem have in Bordeaux?"

"I'm his only one."

"You mean he came here just for you?"

"Sort of."

"Tell me, Mr. Morton," Virgile said, "sorry, Mr. Welling—I can't get your name straight. Please excuse my ignorance, but how does a private sale like this work?"

"It's really very simple," the Englishman explained. "You go to the host's hotel suite. You tell him what you would like to order and how much, and so on. He gives you a price. You can sometimes negotiate a little, but not always. There's a man in the hotel parking garage who will have what you purchased in a vehicle."

"You get it on the same day?"

"About an hour after you've made the purchase."

"Nothing written."

"We are among men of honor, Virgile."

"Certainly, but we don't know this Mr. Wolvertem, and apparently he plans to keep his identity a secret."

"You're right," Welling said, looking a little embarrassed.

Cooker was relishing this discussion. But only a tremor in his nostrils divulged his delight.

No, he would not have any dessert. "Just a coffee. A double espresso for the young man."

Welling declined an after-dinner drink proposed by his friend. He was very focused on satisfying Virgile's somewhat aggressive and unrelenting curiosity.

"What do you intend to buy Mr., uhm, Welling?"

"Ask Benjamin. He knows my weakness for Saint-Émilion. I won't forbid myself a few Médocs or Pomerols."

"So you'll buy out the Angélus."

"Yes, for sure. If there is any, I wouldn't hesitate. Generally speaking, the prices are a good deal, compared with what I've seen recently at the auction houses."

"Which means?" Virgile asked.

"Fifty to sixty euros a bottle for very good years. More, of course, for historic years," Welling whispered.

Cooker took a pen from his jacket and jotted a few figures on the paper tablecloth. Then he ripped off the corner and slipped it to Welling.

"I'll take all the Angélus for the years noted, no matter how much. Then we can split them fifty-fifty if you want."

Welling rubbed his chin, then sighed and sneaked a self-righteous look in Virgile's direction before giving Cooker a wink.

"Do you want a check tonight?" Cooker asked.

"I believe Mr. Wolvertem prefers cash. Actually, I'm sure of it."

"That should be expected, considering his job—if you can call it a job," the winemaker said, drinking the last of his coffee, which was now cold.

"It's what I said, nothing written down," Virgile said, slightly irritated that his boss was condoning this black market.

"Virgile, I'll see you at the office tomorrow around noon," Cooker said, turning to address Welling. "That is, unless you change your mind and accept that he come along for the sale. He knows how to be discreet, you know."

"Benjamin, don't insist," Welling said with some authority. "It's better for our transaction this way."

"You are the best judge of that," Cooker said, taking out his credit card.

"No, let me get this," Welling said, snatching the bill away from Cooker.

Cooker and Virgile said good night to Welling in front of the gates of the city hall without any excess politeness.

"Bye, old chap," Cooker mumbled, wrapping his scarf around his neck.

"Good-bye, Mr. Morton," Virgile said.

As Cooker pulled out his phone to call Elisabeth, a freezing breeze had chased the last night owls away from the Place de Rohan. The cafés had turned off their signs. The Bar de l'Hôtel de Ville was the only place still open, attracting hybrid techno animals who also milled in the deserted Rue de Ruat. High up, the Pey Berland Madonna had to be shivering. Cooker and Virgile would not yet be going home...

11

Night watch. Cooker had to ring several times before a stooped figure shuffled over and agreed to crack open the wrought-iron gate of the Hôtel de Villesèque. An enamel sign above the doorbell read "Logis de France. Traveling sales representatives welcome." The night watchman had messy hair and tired eyes, reflecting many nights on call. Cooker figured he had fallen asleep at the reception desk before having to open the gate. *Can't blame him for being irritated with the two nutcases who wouldn't quit knocking at the window,* Cooker thought.

"Let me see what I have left," the old man said, putting reading glasses on the tip of his beak-like nose.

Only three keys were missing from the board above the man, whose gray Scottish wool sweater gaped at the neck.

"Just one room?" the man asked with a sly smile.

"Two," Cooker said, categorical but polite.

"Will you have breakfast in your room or in the dining room?" the man asked, addressing Cooker.

"Neither, thank you," Cooker said.

"In that case, sirs, may I ask that you pay for your rooms up front, please."

"Certainly," Cooker said, tossing him a credit card.

Virgile stood at the counter and eyed the night watchman write his name in the old-fashioned registry with a black cloth cover.

"Please, two S's in Lanssien."

"Sorry?" the man said.

"My name has two S's," Cooker's assistant said, taking advantage of the moment to glance at the short list of guests in the registry for Thursday, January 28.

Room number twenty-seven listed the name Wolvertem. "Paid" was carefully written in the margin.

"Don't you have any bags?" the watchman asked, handing over two keys with heavy copper plaques engraved "H.V., Bordeaux."

"The man is right," Cooker said. "Why don't we have any bags, Virgile?"

"But boss, you know that—"

"Oh, Virgile, stop justifying yourself. Let's go. I'm exhausted."

The watchman stared as the two men slipped into the elevator after saying a quiet good night. The old hotel clock read one thirty-five. The Rue

Huguerie was in a torpor, which soon caught up with the night watchman. The Hotel de Villeseque's sign was no longer flashing.

Unlocking the door to his room, Cooker flipped the light switch but the orange ceiling fixture didn't go on. Propping open the door so he could see where he was going, Cooker headed to the nightstand and turned on that light. He closed the door, sat down on the squeaky bed, and slipped off his shoes. After straightening the nylon lampshade, he lay down, fully clothed and fell fast asleep.

The walls were so thin, Virgile could hear his boss's regular snoring. It took him a long time to fall asleep between the scratchy, cold, and almost damp cotton sheets. A little before dawn—which a dull concert of street cleaners announced—he started stirring. He finally surrendered to the day when the noise of Cooker washing up in the next room was too jarring to allow him to eek out another fifteen minutes of sleep. After a hot shower, he listened to the day's horror show of news, distilled by an enthusiastic newscaster who made the morning rather ordinary, all in all. This narrow, poorly heated room with gold-flocked wallpaper and disparate furniture was putting him in a bad mood.

Bags under his eyes and his hair still wet, Virgile dressed quickly and went to knock on his employer's door.

135

"Come in. Did you sleep well, Virgile?" Cooker asked without even looking at his ragged assistant.

With his hands behind his back, the winemaker was peering out the window. He was studying the activity on the Rue Huguerie, which was blocked by a traffic jam.

"Not good at all," Virgile said. A tail of his white shirt was hanging out from under his sweater.

"But the hotel was quiet," Cooker said, not turning around.

"That's what you say."

"You've got good timing. Take a look."

Virgile looked out the window. A German station wagon had stopped in front of the hotel garage. The imposing vehicle had a Belgian license plate. Its high top and dark windows made it look like a hearse. Cooker pulled a Churchill from his inside jacket pocket, stuck it between his lips, and lit it with obvious satisfaction.

"You're on, Virgile. Don't let yourself be seen."

The young man had already disappeared down the hallway. Cooker saw the Do Not Disturb sign and smiled. Then he closed the door to his room before calling the reception desk.

"Connect me to Room 27, please."

Virgile chose the service stairs rather than the elevator. Thanks to an untied shoelace, he nearly tripped on the concrete steps when the timed light suddenly went off. The dull sound of an engine, along with the pungent smell of exhaust, confirmed that he had reached the basement. He pushed open the fire escape door and found himself in the parking garage. There were only a few vehicles. The driver of the station wagon had to try twice to park next to a rental van, which bore the unfortunate advertising message "I go for the lowest price." The driver was wearing a raincoat, a russet-colored scarf, and a checked cap. Dark glasses hid a thin face. The man walked slowly but still looked distinguished. Virgile hid behind a pillar so as not to be spotted. The man picked up his pace, then turned around suddenly and examined the parking lot, as if he sensed someone was there. Then he vanished, sucked up by the hotel elevator. Virgile felt for his phone. His breathing was heavy, and he thought he might be trembling. He tried to call Cooker, but he had no reception.

§ § §

"I'm sorry, sir. Room 27 does not answer."

"Are you sure, miss, that you rang Mr. Wolvertem?" Cooker pressed.

"Yes, sir."

"That's okay," Cooker concluded after a moment of silence. "I will try later. Thank you."

The winemaker paced his room, chewing his cigar. He flicked the ashes, not caring about the carpet that absorbed his footsteps. Thick blue swirls of smoke showed his impatience. The Rue Huguerie was busier now. An ambulance siren rose above the concert of horns. The winemaker tried to reach his accomplice, without any luck.

"Jesus," Cooker said.

In a show of anger, he crushed the bulbous cigar that he had lit ten minutes earlier, but it obstinately refused to go out. The reddened tip gave off an aroma reminiscent of the day after a storm, both acidic and refreshing. Why, in his frustration, had he sacrificed such a silky pleasure? Had his Havanophile friend James Welling seen that pitiful act of destruction, he would have certainly thought it a sacrilege.

Virgile stormed into Cooker's room without even knocking. He was out of breath and bumbling.

"So?" Cooker asked.

"So, um—"

"Is he alone?" Cooker said, showing his nervousness.

"Yes. He's wearing a raincoat, a brown scarf, and a kind of cap that you can't find anymore."

"What do you mean?"

"I don't know. Kind of classy but old-fashioned. I mean, your kind of style, boss, if you know what I mean."

"That's a big help," Cooker said, exasperated. "And his shoes?"

"What do you mean, his shoes? I don't know, sir. They were, well—"

"Virgile, you should always look at a man's shoes. They'll tell you more about the person than his tie."

"Oh. He wasn't wearing a tie. That I'm sure of."

"How can you be so sure, Virgile. You told me he was wearing a raincoat and a scarf."

"I don't know. He didn't look like the kind of man who would be wearing a tie."

"Virgile! Good God, who or what did he look like?"

"Calm down, boss. He looked kind of like a cop. You know, the kind of guy you'd see in an American television series. In any case, one thing is certain. He was nervous."

"What do you mean?"

"He was in a hurry and kept looking over his shoulder."

Cooker stared at the tip of the Churchill that was burning slowly in the room's only ashtray. Virgile looked contrite and clumsy, like someone who has been judged wrongly and too quickly. The winemaker pushed up the window that opened onto a ridiculous balcony. He breathed in the city air and listened to the clamoring.

"What are we going to do, sir?" Virgile asked.

"Follow me," was the only response that he got.

Cooker walked purposefully, with Virgile in his wake. They quietly went down a floor and stood in front of the varnished wooden door of room twenty-seven. The winemaker knocked twice. A husky voice answered.

Cooker improvised. "There's a letter for you, Mr. Wolvertem." Virgile was impressed with Cooker's ad-libbing.

The door opened a crack, and the thin shape of James Welling appeared. He was dressed in nothing but a white bathrobe that was too big for him. Cooker, whose size gave him authority, shouldered his way into the room. Virgile followed.

"So, my dear friend, what should I call you now?" Cooker asked. "Morton? Welling? Wolvertem?"

The man was distressingly thin. His knees were knobby, and the tendons on his neck stood out. The top of his hairless chest looked bony. He tried to conceal it by crossing his arms. The man's pale blue eyes looked pathetic. "It's not what you think, Benjamin."

Abandoned on top of the crumpled bed sheets were an off-white Burberry, a cashmere scarf, a gray suit, and a Yves Saint Laurent tie. Cooker went to the bedside table and picked up a bottle of pills that bore the warning "Do not surpass the prescribed dose." He set it back down next to a set of car keys.

Virgile, who was also surveying the room, spotted a pink silk bra on the rug.

"Virgile, go see if the station wagon has what we're looking for. You know my weakness right now. Only Angélus," the winemaker said.

"Fine, boss. But let me check something first."

With a certain arrogance, Virgile gave his employer a serious look before staring into their victim's pitiful eyes.

"Let me explain," the man said.

"You, don't play with me! Is that understood?" Virgile ordered in a voice that stopped the imposter in his tracks. "Boss, we knew the man was quite a wine collector, but I bet he also has a thing for fine call girls. Did you see the pink silk bra on the rug?"

Virgile peered into the bathroom, where a naked woman was trying to hide behind the shower curtain. When she came out in a bathrobe, Cooker couldn't believe his eyes. She had blond hair, blue eyes, high angular cheekbones, and long voluptuous legs. Clearly, the con man had a weakness for not only Bordeaux but also Eastern European women.

§ § §

In the hour that followed, Inspector Barbaroux and his team filled the Hôtel de Villesèque. The cargo in the station wagon was exactly as Cooker had suspected: a few Médocs, some rare Pomerols, a couple of Saint-Émilions, and mostly the stolen Angélus—the best years: 1986, 1989, 1990, 1993, 1994, and the mythic 1995.

Cooker and Virgile gave Inspector Barbaroux a full account of their encounters with the con man, and in return the inspector had let them hang around for the interrogation.

"John the Belgian" was a repeat offender. His impeccable Oxford accent came from his English father, who had been cellar master at Buckingham Palace. His father had married a frivolous redhead from Liège. This singular couple had given birth to twins: Eddy and John. Eddy drowned in the Meuse River when he was eight. John wound up abandoned by his mother, who vanished into the Flemish mist. His cellar master father raised him in London until the father was dismissed after some obscure scandal that brought dishonor to the house of Windsor. The father sank into alcohol and wandering, while his son became a not-very-orthodox trader of fine wines. John the imposter had a reputation as a con artist in Germany and Switzerland, but he and a few recruits fully intended to extend their influence throughout Europe.

The man puffed up his confession with references to Lafite-Rothschild, Prieuré-Lichine, and

Pétrus, along with some Old Testament. But John's good manners did not impress the hardened police officer, who was perhaps a bit rough around the edges.

Morton was handcuffed and invited to change his attitude and drop the masquerade. Barbaroux used language that was as raw as wine straight from the vat: "Stop treating us like jackasses, Mr. Roberton, because we now know your real identity. Your name is John Roberton, and you were born in Canterbury on January 6, 1946. True or false?"

"True, Inspector."

"I'm tempted to believe you. The name Robert Morton was directly inspired by your real name. As for the rest of it—why James Welling and, what was the other one—Wolvertem? Is that Flemish? Perhaps an homage to your mother?"

"Sort of," the accused answered, looking down.

"So, you recruit your accomplices in Belgium, I gather?"

"If you say so."

"I encourage you to be a little more cooperative, Mr. Roberton. You wouldn't want me to use our corkscrew method on you. The bad bottles often end up deep in the cellar. Sometimes they even get forgotten, if you know what I mean."

Roberton was playing with the signet ring, as he did in Cooker's office the day he was supposedly repenting. Then he began a long monologue, punctuated by "Don't you have anything to drink, Inspector?"

Barbaroux invariably responded, "Later, later."

Yes, he was the brains behind the Angélus gang. He had accomplices, musclemen, and others, primarily recruited in Belgium. In Ostend fifteen years earlier, he had met Willem Vanderbroecq, who introduced him to a certain Gerrt Voets, who, until then, had done mostly bank heists. There was far less risk with wines. Their break-ins multiplied as orders came in from collectors around the world.

For some time now, they had worked for an individual named Ignacio Ribera de Montuño. He was a little eccentric and ran a huge family olive-oil business. He lived in a former monastery, now mostly in ruins, in Cienfuegos de las Campanas. The monastery was in a lost hamlet of Andalusia. The millionaire had an insane passion for church bells. His chapel had hundreds of bronze bells that rang out whenever there was a full moon.

The Spaniard was also a great wine connoisseur, frustrated that he didn't have a wine estate of his own. He had made an offer to purchase the Château Angélus estate, which was rejected. Now he was extremely envious of the owner of the grand cru classé Saint-Émilion, and it had turned into an obsession. He wanted to get his hands on all the Angélus he could.

He was very demanding of his Belgian supplier. Unprepared for this customer's new fixation, Roberton had tried to sell him some cases of Clos du Clocher, a very fine Pomerol, but Ignacio would not have it. He wanted Angélus. His terms were strict, and he paid cash.

Willem Vanderbroecq was in charge of finding the wine, and Gerrt Voets was supposed to step in, as needed.

"We didn't know where to find the bottles he wanted," John the Belgian explained. "That's when we started tailing Cooker. That notebook of his is famous for holding secrets. Gerrt Voets planned the carjacking. The kids weren't supposed to hurt the man."

Then Roberton's men robbed the cellars on the Place de la Madeleine in Paris, as well as La Vinothèque de Dionysos in Bordeaux. They had planned a third heist.

Ignacio had a strange sense of humor, and his way of thumbing his nose at the famous Bordeaux wine estate was sending out a cryptic message to coincide with his taking possession of purloined Angélus.

In the meantime, Roberton, ever the opportunist, continued to tail Cooker all the way to La Tortinière. He wanted to meet the man in person.

His Spanish customer insisted on making the exchange in Bordeaux, so Roberton had planned to drive there from La Tortinière. His accomplices would then head to Paris for the final heist. But Roberton had changed his mind at the last minute and had gone looking for Oksana in Tours. That decision threw off their schedule and ended up sabotaging the Paris job.

A young detective was typing out the statement as Barbaroux half-listened to John the Belgian. The deputy came in without knocking, carrying a can of beer.

"Want me to take over, Inspector?"

"No. Sit down. Mr. Roberton is going to serve us up his best and explain how he got rid of his mistress—employee is a better word—in the Loire Valley, along with her lover."

For the first time, the accused dropped his waxy face into his hands.

"Believe me, Inspector, that's not my fault. That was Gerrt. He's the one who found Oksana in Tours. He knew I was hooked on her, and her skipping out had hit me hard. But Gerrt wasn't about to be taken in by her charms. She knew too much, and he didn't hesitate. He killed her, and, to throw the cops off, he made it look like it was the concierge by faking his suicide. The concierge had never even been with her. Gerrt followed him from the hotel on one of his nightly walks and did him in right there on the riverbank."

"Don't try to get out of this, Mr. Roberton. Once you've poured the wine, you have to drink it. And yours seems to be bad two-buck chuck. Now, you said three heists, where was the third?"

"We never got to it because of the Oksana 'incident.' Vanderbroecq took the Morgan to race back to Paris to do it, but didn't make it in time for those crackpot letters. That crazy Ignacio got pissed at us. He cancelled the Châteaux Angélus deal, and decided he wanted a Cave de l'Angélus—that's a rare Swiss wine from the Valais region, purplish robe and leathery aromas. So, there I was, left with all those bottles of wine to unload."

Then he added with a sheepish grin, "I thought Cooker would like them."

Barbaroux booked Roberton. After being held for forty-eight hours, the call girl was released. Although she had Baltic traits, long flowing blond hair, and big Prussian blue eyes, she was really the daughter of a farmer from Corrèze, in the middle of France.

§ § §

The sky looked low. The rainfall that had intensified all day long seemed to be taking a break. The winemakers in Beauséjour, Cheval Blanc,

Belair, Canon, Fourtet, Figeac, Pavie, and Trotte Vieille knew the rain would start up again before nightfall. Yet they had to prune the vines before March first. There was a saying in the Garonne valley. "By the feast of Saint Aubin, prune your vines to shape, and be assured of a plump grape."

The sun was setting, casting its final rays on the hills that overlooked the Landes forest. Workers in dull-green rain jackets were tirelessly removing suckers from the vines. The needle on the barometer fluctuated between rainy and windy. The weather forecasters were predicting a depression over the Bay of Biscay.

Cooker and Virgile were a little late arriving at the Château Angélus, but Hubert de Boüard was not a man to take offense.

"Just in time," their host said loudly when they finally climbed the château's steps. They were soaked from the storm.

Under the large front awning, Hubert congratulated them for so cleverly solving a case that had given him a lot of unasked-for publicity.

Inside the château, he had lined up several bottles that were coming to room temperature not far from a crackling fire in the hearth. Bits of grit were causing occasional mini-explosions, which interrupted the ceremonial silence. The vertical tasting promised to be sumptuous.

At that instant, the church bells of Saint-Émilion rang out the Angélus. Then the bells of the Saint-Martin church responded with equal fervor.

"France's churches are empty. For whom are the Angélus bells ringing?" Virgile asked.

"For God's children like yourself," Benjamin answered. "You know, my boy, wine, like God, is an enigma. You need to taste it many times to make a religion of it. And then—"

"And then, what?" Virgile asked.

"And then, you see, life is nothing but a succession of small miracles. Like this 1989 Angélus that awaits us."

"A miracle, yes," Hubert de Boüard said. "But also a blessing."

Thank you for reading Grand Cru Heist.

We invite you to share your thoughts and reactions on your favorite online platforms.

We appreciate your support.

THE WINEMAKER DETECTIVE SERIES

A total Epicurean immersion in French countryside and gourmet attitude with two expert winemakers turned amateur sleuths gumshoeing around wine country. These titles are already published or coming soon.

Treachery in Bordeaux

The start of this wine plus crime mystery series, this journey to Bordeaux takes readers behind the scenes of a grand cru wine estate that has fallen victim to either negligence or sabotage. World-renowned winemaker turned gentleman detective Benjamin Cooker sets out to find out what happened and why. Who would want to target this esteemed vintner?

www.treacheryinbordeaux.com

Nightmare in Burgundy

The Winemaker Detective leaves his native Bordeaux for Burgundy for a dream wine tasting trip to France's other key wine-making region. Between Beaune, Dijon and Nuits-Saint-Georges, it urns into a troubling nightmare when he stumbles upon a mystery revolving around messages from another era. What do they mean? What dark secrets from the deep past are haunting the

Clos de Vougeot? Does blood need to be shed to sharpen people's memory?

www.nightmareinburgundy.com

Deadly Tasting

A serial killer stalks Bordeaux, signing his crimes with a strange ritual. To understand the wine-related symbolism, the local police call on the famous wine critic Benjamin Cooker. The investigation leads them to the dark hours of France's history, as the mystery thickens among the once-peaceful vineyards of Pomerol.

www.deadlytasting.com

About the Authors

Noël Balen (left) and Jean-Pierre Alaux (right).
(©David Nakache)

Jean-Pierre Alaux and **Noël Balen** came up with the Winemaker Detective over a glass of wine, of course. Jean-Pierre Alaux is a magazine, radio, and television journalist when he is not writing novels in southwestern France. He is a genuine wine and food lover, and won the Antonin Carême prize for his cookbook *La Truffe sur le Soufflé*, which he wrote with the chef Alexis Pélissou. He is the grandson of a winemaker and exhibits a real passion for wine and winemaking. For him, there is no greater common denominator than wine. Coauthor of the series Noël Balen lives in Paris, where he shares his time between writing, making records, and lecturing on music. He plays bass, is a music critic, and has authored a number of books about musicians, in addition to his novel and short-story writing.

ABOUT THE TRANSLATOR

Anne Trager has lived in France for more than 26 years, working in translation, publishing, and communications. In 2011, she woke up one morning and said, "I just can't stand it anymore. There are way too many good books being written in France not reaching a broader audience." That's when she founded Le French Book to translate some of those books into English. The company's motto is "If we love it, we translate it," and Anne loves crime fiction.

DISCOVER MORE BOOKS FROM

LE FRENCH BOOK

www.lefrenchbook.com

The 7th Woman by **Frédérique Molay**

An edge-of-your-seat mystery set in Paris, where beautiful sounding names surround ugly crimes that have Chief of Police Nico Sirsky and his team on tenterhooks.

www.the7thwoman.com

The Paris Lawyer by **Sylvie Granotier**

A psychological thriller set between the sophisticated corridors of Paris and a small backwater in central France, where rolling hills and quiet country life hide dark secrets.

www.theparislawyer.com

The Greenland Breach by **Bernard Besson**

The Arctic ice caps are breaking up. Europe and the East Coast of the United States brace for a tidal wave. A team of freelance spies face a merciless war for control of discoveries that will change the future of humanity.

www.thegreenlandbreach.com

The Bleiberg Project by **David Khara**

Are Hitler's atrocities really over? Find out in this adrenaline-pumping ride to save the world from a conspiracy straight out of the darkest hours of history.

www.thebleibergproject.com

CPSIA information can be obtained at www.ICGtesting.com
Printed in the USA
LVOW04s1454280915

456036LV00015B/671/P

9 781939 474049

[9]